Dog Tags

Heidi Glick

Dog Tags

Contact Information: titleadmin@pelicanbookgroup.com

Cover Art by *Nicola Martinez*

Harbourlight Books, a division of Pelican Ventures, LLC www.pelicanbookgroup.com PO Box 1738 *Aztec, NM * 87410

Harbourlight Books sail and mast logo is a trademark of Pelican Ventures, LLC

Publishing History
First Harbourlight Edition, 2013
Paperback Edition ISBN 978-1-61116-260-8
Electronic Edition ISBN 978-1-61116-259-2
Published in the United States of America

Dedication

I dedicate this book to my father, Jack Mountz, who served as a shining example of Christ's love.

Thank you to my Lord and Savior, Jesus; my husband; my family; my friends; content experts; my critique partners; and Pelican Book Group.

Praise for Dog Tags

In Dog Tags, author Heidi Glick, composes a provocative and compelling novel. This gripping suspense story has well-developed, realistic characters, and a scintillating plot line. I couldn't put it down until I'd finished it!
~Marcy G. Dyer, author of Down and Out.

Breakout author, Heidi Glick, scores with a brilliantly fast-paced romance infused with a mystery that has twists and turns you'll never see coming.
~ Suzanne Hartmann, author of Fast Track Thrillers, Peril and Conspiracy

Heidi Glick accomplished her mission with Dog Tags. Her debut novel is a great mix of suspense, mystery and romance. Mark and Elizabeth are both authentic and delightful as they navigate through secrets and danger on the way to love. Well-researched, beautifully told, Dog Tags is a winner.
~Carole Towriss In the Shadow of Sinai, November 2012

Prologue

The Knight's mind clouded over, like fog settling over the local San Diego metro area. One thing was clear as he sat in his white, sparsely furnished living room: his goal. He must continue his quest to help damsels in distress, ones like Juanita. He hoped she'd listen to him, that she'd understand he only tried to protect her, that she'd appreciate his chivalry. But as he'd learned from experience, the women he chose to rescue might not always be cooperative. Being a knight in shining armor did not always prove an easy task.

The finger in the jar atop the entertainment center served as a reminder: death was far kinder than the fate Juanita could have suffered at the hands of that other man. No matter what society thought, the Knight had done the right thing.

He removed the latex gloves he'd used to handle the jar and hurried over to the stainless steel kitchen sink—spotless and sterile, the way he liked it. He used his foot to open the trashcan and tossed the gloves inside. With great care, three times he washed his hands with antibacterial soap, rubbed them against each other under the warm water, and grabbed a paper towel. Infernal germs lived everywhere. One could never be too careful. Just look at how pneumonia had killed Mom.

His thoughts raced. A bottle of pills sat in the distance. The medication would soothe him, but that could wait. He needed a clear mind for the task ahead.

He released a sigh, sat at his computer, and navigated to the Riversdale Community College website, where he clicked on a picture of the women's basketball team. Using the mouse, he zoomed in closer on the team captain. The next woman he'd help.

Beautiful and helpless. Another fair lady in need of his assistance. Her eyes called out to him, begged him to rescue her.

He opened an image he'd taken of the woman and her wheelchair-bound male friend chatting in the middle of the campus quad. The Knight hit the print button and grabbed the finished page.

A second Internet browser tab allowed him to search the college's website for clues pointing to the woman's major of study: chemistry. So far, she sounded intelligent. Maybe he could help this one without having to resort to drastic measures. He eyed the ammo on the dining table. Still, it didn't hurt to take precautions.

1

Mark Graham closed the book atop his shortened podium. "That's it for today, class. Please read chapters twenty-three through twenty-five for next week."

The afternoon History of Civilizations lecture on ancient fraternal organizations and mysterious societies ended—a topic that never ceased to interest his students. Who didn't love hearing about a good secret? So long as they weren't discussing *his* secrets. He rubbed tired eyes. His secrets would be his undoing. The recurring dream of the ambush had awakened him last night, and he hadn't been able to return to sleep.

Mark packed his lecture notes into his brown leather briefcase, ready to leave Riversdale Community College for the day. As he rolled his wheelchair out of the stucco building, he crossed paths with two brunette female basketball players who took his morning class. They waved, and he continued to the parking lot.

If no one else stopped to chat, maybe he could leave on time for a change, not that it mattered. At thirty-one years of age, he didn't have much to go home to—no wife, no kids, and no prospects. Just a little black dog named Sparky.

Once outside Peterson Hall, Mark undid the top button of his dress shirt and wriggled his tie loose. With his luck, the college would finally relax the dress code a year after retirement. He folded his silk tie and placed it in his briefcase. Order had its place, but he worked alongside junior college students, not businessmen.

He ran his fingers through his hair. Ten years had passed, yet it was strange not to have the standard, Marine-issue haircut. Still, he didn't miss it.

Mark rolled his wheelchair to the faculty parking lot and unlocked his van. New vehicle, new job. He really had made a successful new start. After using a remote to open the right side door of the van, he maneuvered onto his wheelchair ramp, into the driver's side area, and locked his wheelchair in place. He remotely took care of the ramp then tossed his briefcase onto the passenger seat.

He drove south on Pacific Coast Highway, past the naval station, using hand controls to steer the vehicle. With the windows cracked, the chatter of seagulls resonated in the distance.

Mark pulled into the back parking lot of the bait and tackle store he co-owned with two Marine buddies. As much as he wanted to forget his time in the military, Bill and Tim Wilson offered him a job in California near the base where their unit had once been stationed, at a time when he was more than happy to leave his hometown in Ohio. A wooden sign hung slightly crooked in front of Fishy Business. He'd have to get that fixed. Hints of the original brick exterior of the former convenience store peeked out from beneath the newer stucco façade.

Using his wheelchair ramp, Mark exited the van. A slight ocean breeze touched his face. Pretty rare for that time of year. He couldn't complain, as it offered a refreshing break from the dry heat. Salty marine air pervaded as he wheeled through the back door.

Tim Wilson stared out the front window as a young brunette stepped out of an older-model sedan and walked to the pay phone.

Arms crossed, Tim glanced at him. "Who uses a pay phone?"

Mark shrugged. "Guess it's good we haven't had enough dough to completely remodel the place."

"Why not use a cell phone?" Tim continued.

"Maybe it's out of juice. Give the woman a break." Someone that stunning had to have a good reason.

Tim stared out the window again. "Who forgets to charge their phone?"

"Some people are more on top of stuff like that than others." The need to defend her arose, and yet Mark wasn't sure why, except perhaps he hoped she had a good reason. And because he wanted to be the one to find out what it was.

The woman wore flared blue jeans, a white blouse, and brown sandals. The simple outfit complimented her petite frame rather nicely. Tim's type, or so he bragged.

A brunette, eh? Mark cracked his knuckles. He'd better meet her before his friend reached her first. Sure he may be in a wheelchair, but he wasn't dead. Not yet, at least.

He winked at Tim. "While you stand there, I'll go offer my assistance."

"OK, professor, you do that." Tim raised his voice. "Maybe you can enlighten her with facts about the history of the telephone."

"So I'm a history buff. Big deal." Mark went outside. "Excuse me, miss. I couldn't help but notice you used the pay phone."

She looked him in the eyes, as if studying his face,

and stuffed her hands in her pockets. Most looked at the wheelchair and turned away, but she ignored it altogether. "Is there a problem, sir?"

He rubbed his chin. "Well, that's what I was going to ask you. Do you need help with something?"

"Actually, yes. My cell phone's dead, and I left my car charger in my other bag at my apartment." She pushed her pink lips forward into a pout.

Bingo. He'd guessed right. A beautiful damsel in distress. Time to do something about that.

The woman continued. "I needed to make a call to AAA but couldn't get through. Maybe I dialed the wrong number. I have it in my car...somewhere." She walked toward her vehicle. A set of drama masks dangled from her keychain, jingling as she moved.

Thespian. Forgot to charge her cell phone and left the car charger at home. Probably a free spirit. He'd taught long enough to know the type. He followed along behind her. "Sounds like you have car problems. Maybe I can assist you?"

She turned. "Oh, that'd be great. I have a flat tire."

"I'll be right back." Mark went inside, grabbed a cola, and wheeled over to the utility closet. Various chemicals lined the shelves inside. He located a can of tire sealant next to a bottle of glass cleaner. Mark shook his head. Tim's organization of the store shelves proved less than efficient.

Tim swept a nearby section of the commercial-grade floor tile. "Looking for something?"

"Yeah, this." He held up the can of sealant and set it in his lap then went outside and handed the woman the soda. "Here, enjoy this. It might be a while."

"Thanks." She smiled, popped open the top of the can, and took a sip.

Examining her tire, Mark ran his hands along the grooved surface. An object was lodged in a tread near the top of the tire. He pointed it out it to her. "You must have picked up a nail from the road."

As she leaned in closer, she locked eyes with him then glanced away. "That can't be good."

"No, but it's not sticking out too far, so I'll put some sealant on it. Hopefully, that'll give you enough time to get it to a tire shop and get a new tire." Good thing the valve stem sat near the top of the tire. No need to ask Tim for help. Once he removed the nail and the valve cap, he injected the substance inside the valve stem. A scent like permanent marker solvent filled the air. After setting the tire sealant can in his lap, he removed a beige business card from his shirt pocket and handed it to her. "If you have any more problems with the tire before you get to the mechanic, give me a call." He crossed his arms. "Then again, I'm not sure how you're going to call me if your phone's dead. I can follow you to the nearest garage if you'd like."

"Thanks for the offer, but I'll be all right."

Caution to the wind. Fine on her own. Yep, definitely an independent mind.

The woman glanced at the card then scowled as she walked away.

Or maybe she didn't want his help. Perhaps she didn't take kindly to strangers. "Everything OK?"

The woman stopped, held up the card, and turned around. "It says here you're Mark Graham."

"That's right." She appeared to be older than the average Riversdale Community College student—mid-twenties perhaps. But if she did attend there, that made her completely off limits. "Are you taking one of my classes next semester?"

"No."

An attractive woman. Not a student, yet she knew him. Interesting. "Should I know you?"

She gave him a once over. "Nah." The woman began to walk away but stopped. "Mark Graham from Beaumont, Ohio?"

He flinched. His mind searched through memories of all the pretty girls from home, but he drew a blank. "I'm sorry I can't remember your name, though I wish I did." He bit back a grin.

She stretched out her hand to shake his. "Beth...Elizabeth Martindale."

The warmth of her touch jolted him, and it took a moment for her words to register. He studied her face again and factored in for age progression. Those cheekbones, that nose. Yep, a Martindale all right. Heat raced up his cheeks as he remembered his earlier thoughts. Very complicated. She might as well have been a student—definitely in the untouchable, out-of-reach category.

Beth stared at him then at the ground.

Had she noticed the look of fear that must have shown on his face?

"Anyway, thanks." She walked toward her car.

"You're welcome." His mind flashed back to the last time he'd seen Private Martindale, or his sister, for that matter. The only thing about her appearance that might have given away her identity earlier was her slight Midwestern accent, which he recognized the more she spoke. What was she doing here?

Beth rested one hand on the door handle before entering her car. She turned toward him. "I have a question for you. Sort of personal. But you're here, so I might as well ask."

Had she recognized him in front of the Hometown Café, ten years prior? He'd stopped in Beaumont for coffee on his last trip home, but as he'd left, he ran into Beth. Back then, she'd been so young, and she'd given little indication she'd recognized him. Shoot, when he'd first come home from duty, he hardly recognized himself. And she certainly had changed over the years—blossomed into a beautiful woman.

"I ran into Bob Overmeyer in Beaumont a few weeks ago. He told me you were injured trying to save my brother." Beth lowered her voice. "Is that true?"

Leave it to Overmeyer to have such a big mouth. Mark avoided eye contact. How much did she know? His shoulders tensed.

2

The Knight sat in his vehicle during a break and perused the *Riversdale Herald*. The investigation into Juanita Martinez's death ended nine months prior, and yet the Riversdale Police Department was still trying to dig up clues, always one step behind the Knight, or so it appeared. But there were ways of throwing them off.

The afternoon sun coming in through the windshield proved harsh. The Knight flipped down his visor and continued reading. A robbery had taken place at a pawn shop two nights earlier over on Third and Bayshore. The thieves had stolen weapons and ammo. The Riversdale PD investigated and asked for witnesses to come forward with any clues. The Knight finished part of his break-time snack, removed a disposable, prepaid cell phone from his pocket, and dialed the tip hotline. "Hello. I'm calling about the robbery at Surfside Pawn. I was parked nearby when it happened. I saw two, no, make that three, men enter the store. One was Hispanic, one was African American, and one was Caucasian. The Caucasian man was in a wheelchair. Um, he sat outside, probably their lookout man."

"Where were you parked, sir?" a nasally female voice asked.

"Across the street."

"You mean in the parking lot of the grocery store?"

"Uh, yes."

"Did you notice anything else unusual about the men? Happen to see what kind of vehicle they drove?"

"They drove a dark SUV, black or blue. The Hispanic man had tattoos all over his arms. Looked like anchors, sailor type stuff." Being close to the sea, plenty of men should fit the description. That ought to keep Riversdale PD occupied.

"OK, may I have your number in case we need to ask you anything else?"

He ended the call. The cops had what they needed—a trail to follow. As long as the path didn't lead back to the Knight, things were good, and even better if he could cast suspicion on a man in a wheelchair.

He rubbed his arm and remembered the first warning he received when he found his stepdad could walk and used his wheelchair as an excuse. A cigarette burn reminded him not to tell anyone what he'd seen. And the man who'd tried to steal Juanita away, warning her about the Knight—he'd been in a wheelchair, too. So when the basketball team captain smiled while talking to a fellow student who was in a wheelchair, the Knight figured the girl could easily use his help, just as Juanita did. He'd be the one to rescue her from another man in a wheelchair. Even if he couldn't rescue Mom from his stepdad, the Knight could still help other women.

3

Mark's encounter with Beth in front of the café had been long ago. She surely couldn't remember that. Besides, chances were she hadn't recognized him then. Good thing a nonconformist didn't pay attention to detail.

Having stepped away from her car, Beth stood in the parking lot of Fishy Business, a few feet from his wheelchair. The afternoon sun reflected light off a shimmery silver toe ring on her right foot, causing Mark to squint.

Beth sighed. "You never returned to see my family. Never spoke to any of us. It would have been comforting for my mom and dad to know you tried to save their son."

Patrons walked by and waved at him before entering the store—people who didn't know about his failed rescue attempt, and he wanted to keep it that way.

He shrugged and lowered his voice. "Everyone got hurt, right? Am I any better than anyone else?" Sympathy. The last thing he wanted from anyone.

"I appreciate what you did. You put yourself at risk to save my brother. Thank you." Beth bent over and gave him a slight hug. A floral scent wafted in his direction. After thirty seconds of awkward silence, she walked away.

"He would have done the same for me."

Beth turned to face him. "Regardless, you laid down your life for your friend."

Interesting choice of words. "Are you going to be in the area for a while on vacation or…"

"I took a teaching job in Warner's Bay. I found an apartment, but I'm still in the process of moving in."

"Warner's Bay." He scratched his head. "That's about twenty minutes away from here, right?" Was asking a question he already knew the answer to a form of lying? Some sort of deception at least. Quite out of character for him. But fear can make a man do strange things.

She nodded and looked at the ground. "In his letters home, Chris made this area sound exciting." She smiled. "I decided to check it out for myself. Maybe find out more about why he liked it so much."

Moving on a whim. Then again, he'd sort of done the same. But for different reasons. Ones he preferred to keep to himself. "I teach at Riversdale Community College during the day, but on the evenings and weekends, my buddies and I run Fishy Business. The number's on the card I gave you. If you need anything else, let me know. If I can't help, I have friends who can."

Maybe he shouldn't have offered to assist her. In doing so, he might run into Mr. and Mrs. Martindale. What did Beth know about the past, and what might she find out?

Lord, help me.

❧❦

Mark entered the employee restroom, carrying a small duffel bag. Changing out of his work shirt felt good. Afterward, he went to the back of the store, opened the lid on the bait freezer, and inhaled. Chum, sweet chum. He chuckled and set his bag on the floor by his desk then began to review the company books. Lucky him—being elected to manage the company finances. But at least his math skills had given Bill and Tim a reason to partner with him. Mark manually performed several calculations and recorded them. He scratched his head for a moment and smiled. No reason to complain. Business was good.

He sniffed. Nacho cheese. That could only mean one thing—Tim was nearby.

"What kept you so long?" Tim asked. "The night crawlers have been restless without you here."

Mark kept his head in the books, entered a number into his calculator, then proofed it against a number in the ledger to ensure he'd entered it correctly. When did Dalton invent the modern calculator—1902? Mark set down the calculator, turned to face his two friends and attempted to take an interest. "The night crawlers? Restless? Really?"

"That's a joke." Tim held a bag of chips in one hand and wiped his cheese-covered hand on his denim shorts.

Mark raised an eyebrow. It wouldn't hurt Tim to at least try to prevent crumbs from falling on the floor.

Bill Wilson stood nearby at the register, perusing a comic book. "If that was a joke, then it was a lousy one."

Mark grinned as Tim flashed Bill a dirty look. How could two brothers be so different? "I knew our stranded traveler, so we chatted for a while."

"A student from Riversdale?" Tim asked. "Because you can't date students, but you could introduce her to me. She is one, isn't she? Does she play sports? Volleyball? Basketball?"

Could Tim think about anything other than food, fishing, or women? Mark sighed and shook his head. "Someone from back home." He didn't have to specify who.

The snack vending truck pulled into the driveway as Tim munched on more nacho cheese-flavored chips.

"Does she need help with anything?" Bill asked.

The door opened, and a bell announced the presence of Randy, the snack vendor. The lanky man entered, bringing in products to restock the store. Mark held his ledger away from his face and squinted. Time to restock again already? He wheeled over to the counter and picked up a pair of reading glasses then moved back to his desk. "I fixed her tire. She didn't say she needed anything else, so I assume we won't be hearing from her." He reached into his pocket for his cell phone and ensured it was turned on. Just in case.

Tim tilted his head. "Your hometown was pretty small, wasn't it?" He popped a chip in his mouth.

Mark peered at Tim over the top of the books. "And your point is?"

His friend shrugged and finished munching his chip. "What are the chances of running into someone from back home?"

"Well, and someone related..." Mark bit his lip. It was too late to reel the words back into his mouth like a large kelp bass on a line.

Tim's hazel eyes widened, providing a stark contrast with his ginger-colored mop. "Related to...?"

Mark clenched his jaw.

His friend took a break from his chip fest for a moment. "Details, I want details."

Mark glanced at his ledger and continued performing his calculation. He lowered his voice. "She's Chris's sister."

Tim stuffed another chip in his mouth and crunched it quickly. "Chris?"

Randy handed Bill an invoice and left. Bill reviewed it and scratched his sandy blond hair.

Tim raised his voice, "As in Private Chris Martindale? His younger sister?"

"That's the one. I gave her my card, and she recognized my name." He looked up from his ledger, staring off in the distance. "At first, I thought she was a student, and maybe that's why she recognized me."

Bill turned toward Tim, arms crossed over his sci-fi t-shirt. "I didn't know Martindale had a sister."

Tim nodded and licked his cheese-covered fingers. "Yeah, I remember him getting letters from her."

No reason he couldn't work outside. Mark rolled his chair through the door, and though Tim and Bill's voices faded, he could still make them out.

"Will you look at that?" Bill said. "He went out back to get more night crawlers."

"So what?" Tim crunched his chips.

"So he tried to save Chris but couldn't. You know he doesn't like to talk about it, tends to bring on his, you know"— Bill lowered his voice—"episodes. Change the subject when he comes back."

Mark returned. "It's a thin door. I could still hear you, you know, even despite my...episodes." He wheeled over and picked up the books. Once back outside, he went over to a picnic table and examined the store's financial records. Hadn't he come to Riversdale to forget the past? Out of all the people he could have run into, it had to be Martindale's sister.

And so pretty, too.

Why Lord?

Especially in the midst of one of his episodes— amazing how things that took place during the ambush still affected him physically and mentally. Everything was fine until the last month or so, until he came across a picture of him and Chris from high school. Then the nightmares returned.

Mark's students, many of his university coworkers, and even neighbors had no knowledge of the ambush. He shared the information on a need-to-know basis. Maybe they assumed he had multiple sclerosis or some other malady. For now, he didn't know and didn't care as long as the details of the past remained buried like hidden land mines.

He gazed off in the distance and leaned his head on his hand. Over time, he had learned to trust God more and rely less on his own reasoning. Maybe God placed Beth in his path for a reason. Perhaps He'd be so kind as to share the reason with Mark.

❧◦❧

Beth drove toward her apartment, picked up her car charger, and began charging her cell before heading toward the storage facility. Turning left out of her complex, she realized the storage facility was in the other direction. Her blast from the past with Mark distracted her too much. She debated whether their reunion was a good thing.

She had to go straight for a few more miles but couldn't remember the name of the street where she needed to turn. At least, she'd written down the address. She stopped at a red light and fumbled through her purse to find the scrap of paper with the address. The light turned green. A horn honked behind her. Beth looked up and continued driving. Maybe she could stop at the next light. Or perhaps she could remember something about the place. A sign with a giant burger came to mind. John's Jumbo Burgers. The storage facility was near the fast food chain.

Beth's dad had helped her move her stuff in a moving truck then dropped everything off at a storage facility until she found an apartment. She'd upset him with her plan to move her things herself. Mom understood, at least.

There was no way Beth was going to fit all her stuff in her tiny car. If Chris were alive, things would have been much easier. He would have helped her in an instant, assuming he stayed in one place that long. But like her, chances were he would have gotten bored and wanted to move on. Which is why she'd moved in the first place—for a change in scenery. She'd lived in the same small town her entire life. But California was a different story. The place was home to Hollywood and amusement parks, the beach, the mountains, and the desert. The Golden State was full of excitement. And no winter snow fell in Riversdale.

The big, colorful giant burger sign lie ahead. Bingo. She hung a right and pulled into the driveway of the storage facility. Which one was hers? B something—B98.

She parked and fumbled through her purse three times before finding the key to the padlock. Aha! She whisked it out, opened the lock, then pulled the handle on the door and attempted to shove it upward to open it further. If only she were taller. At least she opened it most of the way.

Beth walked toward a dresser next to the wall and pulled. When it didn't move, she tugged again. A sharp pain rushed down her back. She climbed behind the piece and tried to push it, moving it just a few inches. As her lower back muscles pulsated, she slumped down against the side of the wall and sat on the concrete then reached into her bag and grabbed her cell phone. Next to it sat Mark's card. She flipped it over. He'd said his friends could help even if he couldn't.

Her mind flashed back to eighth grade. No way. Someone else could help her. Not Mark, not after his reaction to the note from long ago. But who else did she know in town well enough to call for help?

Beth stood and winced then yanked on the storage door to close it. There was no sense in losing all her junk. She replaced the padlock on the door and hobbled back to her car. Though the initial movement into the car proved most painful, the ride back to her place was not as bad as she feared.

She pulled into her apartment and noticed her landlord walking by her neighbor's door. "Is Marisa home?" Beth asked.

"No."

So much for asking Marisa for help.

Beth could call her dad, but then he'd lecture her about her impulsivity. Nope, she had to figure this one out on her own.

She took a deep breath. Eighth grade and the Valentine's Day debacle happened long ago. Maybe too long ago for Mark to remember. And besides, she couldn't remain angry with him forever. When God said to forgive seventy times seven, she supposed that included Mark, too. Beth entered her apartment and slouched onto her couch. She opened her bag and removed her cell phone and Mark's card. Someone from back home. Better than no one. She stared at the phone, then the card, then the phone again, as if waiting would change her circumstances.

ৡৢৎ

Mark continued to review the books. His cell phone rang, and he looked at the time before answering. An hour and a half had slipped by. He removed his phone from his pants pocket and glanced at the caller ID. Maybe a sales call. Still, he answered it. A chattering gull flew overhead. Mark held his phone to his right ear and covered his left ear.

"Are you still offering your assistance?" Beth asked.

He cleared his throat and managed a nervous laugh. "I wouldn't have given out my number otherwise."

"I need to move some furniture. Do you think some of your friends could help?"

Mark looked down at his stomach. The last time barracudas swam in his gut had been before the ambush. Perhaps not a good sign. "Are we moving a few small boxes or something larger?"

"Some boxes but also some furniture."

He grabbed his pen. "I'll call a friend to help with the larger stuff. I can get the boxes. What's your address?"

"121 West Balboa Street, Apartment B-13, Warner's Bay."

Mark scanned his books but didn't have any scrap paper handy. He jotted the number down on his hand.

"Balboa Street? Named after Vasco Núñez de Balboa."

"Yeah, I guess so."

"See you in about twenty minutes." He grabbed the books and took them back inside. Turning, he wheeled toward the back door, again detecting the faint scent of nacho cheese.

"Where are you going?" Tim asked.

"Out—probably for the rest of the day." He didn't need to explain his whereabouts to everyone. Then again, it might have been fun to add "and with a girl" just to see Tim's reaction. But that would only bring on more questions. Mark left the store and wheeled his chair into his van. Once inside the vehicle, he put on his sunglasses and looked at his hand: 121 West Balboa Street. He breathed a sigh of relief. Balboa was far from Oleander Avenue, which meant less chance of being recognized and fewer questions. He punched the address into his GPS and entered the freeway, driving toward Warner's Bay.

He shook his head. Perhaps this was a bad idea and would prolong his current episode. He was in no mood to talk to a shrink about his condition. What was God trying to show him through all this?

Mark pulled up to the Playa Del Sol apartment complex. There was no guard station, so he drove directly into the main parking lot, unannounced and unnoticed. Traffic roared in the distance. Who could sleep with all that noise? Four adobe-colored stucco-adorned buildings stood before him, framed by a plethora of queen palms and pink and white oleander. He located building B then Beth's apartment. Number 13. Good thing he didn't believe in superstitions.

Mark approached her door and wondered what Chris would have done. He'd probably be concerned about Beth's safety. Maybe Mark should look after her. It wouldn't be hard for him to check in on her from time to time. He rapped on the door.

She answered his knock in a hurry and greeted him with a smile.

After exchanging pleasantries, Mark examined her door. He pointed at the bent and battered strike plate. "Is your father around? This should be beefed up a little." No way would the man allow his daughter to live in a non-gated community with a flimsy door lock.

Mark breathed a slight sigh of relief, knowing if the man wasn't around, at least that meant no chats with the Martindales. He liked them well enough, but he didn't need to see them, didn't want their pity. "This lock is useless. I'm no cat burglar, but even I could pick this with a credit card. We can go to a hardware store and get you a new one."

Beth tilted her head. "Or I could mention it to the landlord. Whatever you think."

He noticed a slight limp as she walked away. "You OK?"

"Yeah, I tried to move something on my own. Bad idea. Hurt my back a little."

Mark followed her inside. Walls coated in flat white paint enclosed the dinky apartment. Just the thought of the grainy texture set him on edge, like nails on a chalkboard. In the center of the living room, against the far wall, stood a grayish blue couch and a small, oval coffee table made from oak-veneered particle board. Dorm-room furniture.

A musty smell filled the space but lessened as he neared Beth, the scent replaced with her floral perfume—just right, not too overpowering.

Boxes and posters cluttered her apartment. One

wall sported a theatrical poster for a Broadway musical. He spied a copy of the *Buckeye*. "I see you brought your yearbooks with you. Say, what year is that? That's not my senior year, is it?" He began to reach for it.

Beth bent over, picked up the book, and shoved it into a box. "No, I don't think so. Sorry."

Mark lifted his eyebrows. She'd moved toward that yearbook with surprising quickness.

A large, dark brown teddy bear in a purple vest peered from another box. "Do you remember when your brother and I built a fort and you tried to bring your stuffed animals in there, and we chased you out?"

Beth grinned. "I hadn't thought about that in years. I'd like to think this place is a little bit nicer than that fort. It's definitely small, but at least it's in a relatively safe neighborhood."

Relatively safe. Good choice of words. He pulled back a living room window curtain and stared at the vehicles parked outside Beth's building. No bars framed the inside windows. A good sign.

A lively song played from upstairs, but Mark didn't recognize the tune. Stuff his students might listen to. It sounded like the radio sat in another room of Beth's apartment. He remembered why he'd saved up and purchased his own home—peace and quiet.

"I think I'll like it here. Always lots of people going in and out. Seems like there will never be a dull moment."

So she liked all the noise and commotion? He closed the curtain and faced Beth.

Beth stood, hands on her hips, and grinned. "I hope your friends at the bait shop don't mind me borrowing you."

He shook his head. "Too bad if they do. I'm a little miffed with them right now."

"Oh. Why's that?"

"They mean well. But they're worried I'll have a flashback about Chris's death because you and I ran into each other."

Beth's eyes appeared to convey concern. "And you're not, right?"

"It's been eleven years." Eleven years, two months, five days. He stared at the tops of his gray tennis shoes and lowered his voice. "I don't have flashbacks like I used to." He hadn't jumped at a car backfire in years.

Mark spied a dark blue Bible sitting on top of a box. "Still, there's this part of me that feels…"

Beth leaned toward him. Her chocolate brown eyes met his. "Feels what?"

He moved away from her and closer to the Bible then played with the book's tattered edges. What *did* he feel? "Bad, guilty, sad, I don't know—something. I found God, and I was going to talk to Chris, but then it was too late." Some friend he'd been. He tried to save Chris physically, when he should have tried harder to save him spiritually. He hung his head. Maybe this would further aggravate his current episode. If he could help Beth move her stuff and go on his way, do his good deed and split, then maybe he'd be all right.

Beth inched closer, moved her arm toward his shoulder, but stopped short of touching him. Perhaps realizing the awkwardness of the situation unfolding, she quickly crossed her arms. "If it's any consolation, I tried to talk to Chris about God."

"I was going to ask you about your Bible since none of us attended church much growing up. Looks like you found God, too?"

She nodded. "Yeah, me and my parents."

Hope stirred inside of him. Beth was a Christian and had shared the Gospel with Chris, too. Same hometown. Same faith. "So what did Chris say?"

Beth gazed downward. "He kept putting things off." She flopped onto the couch.

Not what Mark wanted to hear. He wheeled next to her and gazed into her eyes. Her beautiful, brilliant eyes. "It's not your fault."

She looked away and twirled her shoulder-length hair with her fingers. "I never thought it was."

"Really? You never feel—"

Beth shook her head. "No, everyone has to decide for themselves."

"True." He folded his hands. "When I tried to talk to Chris, he always wanted to discuss things later. Maybe I should have pushed it more." He fixed his gaze on the ground.

"You say it's not my fault, but something tells me you have trouble wrapping your mind around the concept."

Why were they still talking about the past? "Are you always this verbose? Oh, wait. I remember when you were little. Yes, you always have been." What a chatterbox. He attempted to contain a smile.

She scowled then grinned. "Not fair, Mr. Graham."

"*Mr.* Graham?" Only students referred to him that way.

Beth nodded. "Yeah, you're old now. I can call you mister."

"Old? Ouch!" Maybe the wheelchair added a few years.

She stood, arms crossed. "I know, and I asked you to help move furniture." She raised an eyebrow; a mischievous look formed on her face. "Is that elder abuse?"

Was this her way of flirting? He bit back a grin. "You're enjoying this."

"I am. It's not as if"—Beth stared into the distance—"not as if I can tease Chris anymore."

He cleared his throat. "About the furniture...?"

Beth's countenance changed. "Yes, the furniture is at a storage facility. I guess we should head out."

"I called my teaching assistant, and he's going to meet us there with his SUV. I just need to call him with the location. I can help with boxes. Anything larger, I'll let him carry."

She grabbed her purse and keys, and he followed her out the door. Once outside, they entered his van and drove off to retrieve her belongings from storage.

A half a mile away, at a stoplight, Mark rubbed his head. Maybe Tim and Bill weren't the only ones he could confide in. Beth had been so easy to talk to. Perhaps he could sit her down and explain things.

He shook his head and, using his hand controls, accelerated his vehicle. Nope. This was not the time for confessions. Help the damsel in distress and get on with life. Complete the mission.

ॐ∘ॐ

Within twenty minutes, Mark pulled up in front of the Seaside Storage Facility. It looked like every other storage place he'd ever seen, with the exception of the fluorescent-painted siding. He continued a tenth of a mile from the entrance to get to her storage unit. Just before getting out of the vehicle, he shot a double take at Beth. Chris's sister. His *younger* sister. And Mark needed to remember that. He pictured her wearing pigtails and braces. From now on, whenever he'd see her, he would keep that image etched in his memory—that ought to help.

Mark exited his vehicle and examined the exterior of Beth's storage unit. During his time in the Marines, he'd lived in smaller places. She couldn't have that much stuff. He just hoped she hadn't tossed everything into one giant box like Chris would have done. For best friends, he and Chris were opposites. Private Chaos and Corporal Neat Freak. Despite their differences, they managed to remain friends, probably because they were so different. Watching Beth dig through her purse further confirmed she and Chris were related. In all the time he'd known Chris, he could never find anything he owned easily.

The scent of paint lingered. Using his fingers, Mark examined the outside of the storage unit. Dry. Maybe it'd been painted a few days earlier. Guess there'd been a sale on chartreuse paint.

Though close to setting, the late afternoon sun brought out the highlights in Beth's hair. She'd had perfectly fine dark brown hair before. He shook his head.

An older black SUV pulled up next to Mark's van. His teaching assistant, Kevin, and another guy stepped out of the vehicle. Mark waved to Kevin. Maybe he should invite Kevin to the store and invite Beth to join him, so the two could get to know one another. Someone younger and more mobile. That had to be whom she would prefer.

Kevin gestured to the guy standing next to him.

"This is Will. You may have seen him on campus. He's a transfer student. Anyway, he's going to help, too."

Mark reached out his hand to shake Will's. "Thanks for coming."

"No problem."

Beth removed a key from her purse. "Aha. Here it is."

Mark stifled a sigh.

After unlocking the padlock on the unit door, Beth stepped back, allowing Kevin to lift the door and roll it toward the ceiling. Boxes lined the outer walls. Furniture took up the rest of the space. Entering the unit, Beth reached for a box.

Mark stretched out his hand, like when she'd tried to walk on a frozen pond years earlier, and he and Chris had to stop her. "Spiders. Watch out. We do have quite a few black widows around here."

She nodded. "Good to know."

Mark and Beth spent ten minutes moving various smaller boxes from the outer edges of the storage facility into the van while Will and Kevin moved larger items.

Beth looked at the outside of a larger box, carried it from the storage unit to Kevin's SUV, placed it down on the ground, and ripped it open.

Mark rolled closer to inspect the contents: Classic movie DVDs. So she liked older things. Not what he would have expected.

Beth picked one up, stared at the cover for a moment, and then tossed it back in the box. "So you teach history?"

Mark loaded the box into the back of the SUV. "History of"—Dare he say it—"Ancient Civilizations."

She chuckled. "Right up your alley."

"And then of course, I have my glamorous job at Fishy Business."

She grinned. "I love the name, by the way."

No, no, she shouldn't. Beth shouldn't love anything related to him.

"Thanks. I came up with it." he said instead. "And how about you? What do you teach?" He moved around the storage unit, surveying what was left. No way she could convince him she needed all of this. Just not possible. He wheeled toward a rectangular, white kitchen table near the middle of the unit.

Beth walked over and reached for one end of the table. "English and drama to middle schoolers."

Will stepped in and grabbed the other end.

"Middle school? All that energy, all those raging hormones. Yikes, better you than me." Sweat began to bead on Mark's brow. Too bad he hadn't worn shorts. He couldn't wait for summer to end and fall to begin.

Beth positioned her hands around the end of the table several times before finding the right grip. She picked up her end. "Oh, yeah, right. It's been quite a few years since you were in middle school."

She really was going to play the age thing up. Was she flirting or just plain teasing? It was hard to tell.

Will picked up his end, and he and Beth moved the table toward the SUV.

"OK, let's settle this. So remind me, how old are you?" Mark asked.

Once in front of the SUV, she set down her end of the table and chuckled. "Twenty-six."

Will set down his end and stepped inside the SUV.

Mark shrugged. "So I'm thirty-one."

She glanced up at him and smiled, using her hand to shield her eyes from the sun. "Hey, to me, anyone over thirty is ancient."

Will smirked.

Ouch. He had no chance of winning this argument. Maybe his best bet was to change the subject. "So it's August, and while I'm teaching summer school, I'm guessing you haven't started teaching yet."

Kevin came over and helped Will lift the table into the SUV.

"No, not for three more weeks." Beth sighed. "And even then, I don't get paid until the middle of the following month. Some sort of payroll thing."

He did the math in his head. "That's five weeks away."

"I know. I haven't told my dad yet. He won't be happy. I'll have to listen to one of his lectures. I have some money saved up from my last job, but I suppose it wouldn't hurt to find a part-time job, at least until school starts."

He leaned closer. Beth's eyes reminded him of her old man. "How is your father?"

She walked over and picked up another box. "The same, only he and Mom talk about retirement more often." Beth shook her head. "Who does he think he's kidding? He loves to work."

Mark picked up a large sealed paper box and placed it on his lap. "Your dad's a good man. When my father died, your dad made sure I attended little league. And on Chris's fifteenth birthday, your dad took us to see the Cleveland Indians. What a game. I still have the ticket stub at home. The Indians beat the Angels, four to three." He breathed deeply, trying to remember the smell of the hot dogs. A nice gesture by Mr. Martindale.

And just that quickly, guilt and shame from a failed rescue attempt overtook him. Mark slumped his shoulders.

Beth set the box in the SUV. "Oh, I remember that. The two of you talked about it afterwards for weeks."

Mark stared at her. The Martindales always helped him. Perhaps this was his chance to return the favor. Maybe even a chance to make up for past transgressions. "Tim and Bill, they're my business partners. Lately, Tim's been complaining we need to review our inventory. Maybe we could hire you temporarily."

Her eyes widened. "Me? Work for you?"

Mark set his box in the SUV. "I think it's a great idea—employing youth to help out the old folks. Or you could wait to talk to your dad about your problems."

"Maybe it's not such a bad idea after all." Beth rubbed her neck and lowered her voice. "Thanks."

He'd offered to give her a job. What happened to helping her move and then going home? If he'd kept his mouth shut...What if she pried? "Ready to move the rest?"

"Sure."

Kevin and Will picked up an olive green and brown bed frame and carried it toward the SUV.

Mark stuck out his left hand and gestured toward the item. "Beth, why is your bed painted in camouflage?"

"My dad had trouble taking apart my four poster bed, so this is Chris's. Made it easier to move."

On second glance, the frame did appear familiar. He remembered it from Chris's room. "I'm glad your parents can move stuff around. When my mom died, I tried moving some of her things. Seemed too hard so I had the realtor sell the place and send me the rest of her belongings."

"I forgot your mom passed away. Not too long after Chris died, right?"

"One year later. I came home briefly."

Beth studied his appearance then scowled. "That *was* you."

"What do you mean?" He looked away from her, unable to bear her scrutiny.

She pointed at him. "Years ago. I passed you in front of the Hometown Cafe."

He hung his head. "I—"

"You didn't stop to say hi." She bit her lip. "What happened? You didn't recognize me, or…?"

He lowered his tone. "It's complicated."

Will and Kevin closed the back of the SUV and approached him.

Mark extended his hand. "Will, nice to meet you. Thanks for coming and helping, guys."

Will shook his hand. "If you don't mind, I'm going to head back to the car and take a pill. I feel a headache coming on."

"Sorry to hear that," Mark said.

Kevin took a step toward him. "You're welcome, Mr. G." Kevin reached out to half slap, half shake Mark's hand.

Mark did the same, slapping two twenties in Kevin's hand.

"Will and I can follow you and help unload," Kevin said.

"That would be great, thanks. Although, are you sure your friend will be OK?"

"Yeah. He gets migraines. At least that's what he

claims the pills are for. Sure takes a lot of 'em. Anyway, we're headed to a Riversdale women's basketball game this evening, but we should be able to help you and still make it on time."

Kevin and Will got in the SUV and followed Mark and Beth to her place.

Once they unloaded all the furniture, Kevin and Will left.

Mark stayed behind. He glanced at his watch then at Beth. "Look, it's almost six o'clock. Would you like to eat?" Did he just invite her to dinner? This was not part of his original plan to help her and then avoid further contact. Talk about a case of word vomit.

Beth crossed her arms then relaxed them at her sides. "Yeah, I'm starving. Where are we going?" For someone who had been a little disappointed with him earlier, she'd sure changed her tune. A good sign.

He moved closer. "This great place in Riversdale."

They stepped outside the apartment. Beth closed the door behind them and locked it.

Mark wheeled toward the driver's side of the van. One harmless dinner. A nice gesture. What could it hurt?

4

The Knight sat at the dinner table and finished reading a newspaper article about unemployment. The economy was down, and crime was up. The Riversdale PD remained busy, keeping the streets of Riversdale safe. As long as the police stayed occupied, the Knight could conduct business as usual. Being his day off, he saw no need in taking his pills. No coworkers or acquaintances around. No need to stage an act.

He stood and removed a yellow memo pad from his desk drawer and wrote "store list" at the top, followed by several items: candles, matches, candy-coated chocolates, hand wipes, paper towels, bleach, antibacterial soap, incense, picture frame, notebook.

Returning to the table, the Knight opened a package of candy and scattered them, sorting them by color. Next, he counted. Eight yellow. Twelve green. Ten red. Ten orange. Eight dark brown. How he missed the light brown ones. Why they'd stopped making those and added in the blue ones, he'd never know. Speaking of blue, he counted eleven of them. An odd number. Unacceptable. He picked up a blue candy and walked out to his garage. Clenching his teeth, he grabbed a hammer and set the lone chocolate candy on his tool bench. Holding the hammer in position, he brought it down upon the chocolate and smashed it. After returning the hammer to its proper place, he went back to the house, resumed his seat, and spread the living section of the *Riversdale Herald* across the table, yet three inches from his candy. They shouldn't touch.

On the third page of the section, an advertisement announced fall registration of local schools. The ad included photos of new teachers in the surrounding districts. While he liked searching out women in need, it was better when they came to him. He scanned the pictures. His right temple pounded, and he massaged it. He gazed at the last photo on the page. Beth Martindale. Warner's Bay Middle School. A future project, perhaps?

Another one in need. Though maybe too close to home. Perhaps he needed to concentrate on helping ladies in the next county, in a locale outside of the Riversdale PD's jurisdiction.

5

Beth rode back with Mark to his house—a small, Mission-style home. Talk about pueblo flair. Orange Spanish tile on the roof, and inside, terra cotta floor tile with what appeared to be the original dark woodwork on the interior. Massive overhead beams framed the ceiling. A sense of style for a former jock. Not how she envisioned his house, but then what did she expect it to look like?

Here she was standing inside Mark Graham's house—not where she would have guessed she'd have been had someone asked her years earlier. She examined her hair in the stained glass mirror next to the door and adjusted several out-of-place strands. They'd been moving furniture all day. How long had it looked like that?

An aging Hispanic woman greeted them in the foyer. "*Hola*, Mark."

The scent of glass cleaner mixed with disinfectant permeated the air. A change in pace from the lemon furniture polish scent of her childhood home. Glass cleaner and disinfectant—maybe that's what Mark's house smelled like growing up. Not that she could remember going to his house. Perhaps once or twice she studied the outside of his home when her father drove Mark over there and dropped him off. No, all their encounters had taken place at school or her home. Outside of those places, she didn't know much about him.

Mark moved forward toward the entryway. "Hello, Lupe. You're not on your way out, are you?"

"*Sí*, I was. You need me to do something else?"

"This is my friend, Beth." Mark turned and gestured toward her. "Beth, this is my housekeeper, Lupe." He looked at Lupe. "I was hoping you'd stay and enjoy dinner with us, or are you in a hurry to get home?"

The woman scrunched her face. "My husband works second shift this month. No hurry." Lupe studied Beth for a moment and grinned.

"Nice to meet you." Beth extended her hand. It was good Mark had someone to help him out.

Lupe shook Beth's hand, wide-eyed. "*Sí*. Nice to meet you." She turned toward Mark and winked. "Mark, do you want me to cook for you?"

"I can manage, thank you. No, Lupe, you're off the clock. Tonight, you're my guest."

Smiling, Lupe moved to one side and allowed a small black dog to scamper past and jump into Mark's lap.

Mark scratched the dog's head, wheeled to his sliding glass door, and let the dog outside. Mark shut the door and pointed outside at the dog. The animal spun in circles, chasing its tail. "That's Sparky. I found him back in Beaumont."

Beaumont, Ohio—their connection. No way around it.

Beth placed her hands in her pockets. "Sparky, how original. I'm guessing you narrowed down name choices to either that or Spot?" Why hadn't he laughed at her joke? It wouldn't hurt the corporal to smile a little. Perhaps sarcasm was against Marine regulations.

She stopped to observe the dog for a moment. "Actually, it's a cute dog. Kind of looks like a little black wolf. What breed is that?"

"He's a Schipperke. Most of them have their tails docked. But I'm glad his isn't. I think it adds character."

She wrinkled her forehead. "A Schipperke? I never heard of that breed before."

"LBDs. Little Belgian dogs, little barge dogs, or little black devils, depending on how they're behaving. The Belgian resistance used them in World War II to relay messages."

"Little black devils?" She stared at Mark. "Is it safe to pet him?"

"I don't know." Mark opened the door, letting Sparky inside. "Have *you* had your rabies shot?"

"Ha, ha." Beth whistled, and the dog came right to her. She crouched down and scratched his head. Sparky wagged his curly black tail and flashed a huge grin. His incisors gleamed. "Whoa, nice teeth there, little fella'." Beth stood up and stepped away from the dog.

"It's OK. He doesn't bite."

"That's good to know." Good to know, and yet being bitten by the dog was the least of her worries. Beth petted Sparky and then glanced at Mark. "So, you…you're making dinner?"

He wheeled toward the kitchen. "While my Mom worked, I learned to cook."

"Interesting. I'm sure it will be great." Her palate anticipated a microwaveable frozen dinner.

He returned with a plate on his lap. "I'll fire up the grill."

"Can I do anything to help?"

"You can set the table."

She made two attempts to locate the silverware drawer. Everything in the kitchen was positioned at a level Mark could reach from his chair. From the looks of his place, he hadn't kept many memories from home. He and Chris had been best friends growing up. It was a little odd he wouldn't put out one photo of them together. Then again, maybe he was trying to move on. She clasped the chain around her neck. Maybe someday she could do the same.

Lupe entered the kitchen. "Let me. I know where he keeps things." She waved her hand at Beth. "You go outside."

"Are you sure?"

Lupe shooed her with both hands. "*Sí*. Go on now."

Mark looked puzzled as Beth walked outside.

She shrugged. "Lupe wanted me to keep you company."

"That sounds about right," Mark muttered under his breath.

Sparky ran over to greet Beth. She knelt to pet the dog's head and lowered her voice. "Between you and me, Sparky, I think he's going to poison us." The dog stared at her and panted, giving the appearance of grinning.

Mark wheeled over to where she stood and pointed at her. "I heard that."

She stood up. "You have a nice house, a nice vehicle, nice furniture, nice dog"—Beth crossed her arms—"with my apartment, I feel like I'm just playing grown up."

"Yep."

Her neck muscles tensed. "You didn't have to

agree." Beth found a tennis ball in the yard and tossed it to Sparky. He seemed to enjoy the game.

Mark turned foil packages on the grill. "So why'd you change your hair?"

"Huh?"

"The highlights."

She held a strand of her hair and examined it. "What's wrong with them?"

Mark shrugged. "Nothing. I guess I don't understand what was wrong with your hair before."

"That's because you're a guy." He'd noticed. That couldn't be all bad. Then again, Mark Graham always proved to be a tough one to figure out.

Beth followed as Mark wheeled back inside and placed a plate of grilled vegetables and meat on the table.

"Lupe, *somos listos por comer*. Time to eat."

"You speak Spanish?" Beth asked.

Mark arched his brow. "You?"

"Just my two years of required foreign language at Beaumont High. I might be able to ask where the bathroom is. Stuff like that."

"If you ever want to brush up on your Spanish, Lupe and I are glad to help."

"Thanks for the offer." Beth sat at the table. Chris wasn't there for her. Lupe would have to serve as a buffer.

Her mind raced to think of ways to break the awkward silence. "So do we pray and recite some Marine creed or just shout 'Semper Fi'?"

Mark glared at her.

Her jaw dropped. "You gave me the 'Jim look.'"

Mark smirked.

"You know what I mean. That look my dad used

to give. You know the one."

"Shall we?" He prayed then placed his napkin on his lap.

Beth pointed at him. "That look. Don't do that again. It's creepy. No wonder people listened to you in the military. One look and...uggh." She shivered.

Mark chuckled and sipped his water then moved his napkin aside and patted his lap. Sparky jumped up.

Beth stabbed a piece of meat with her fork. "You let your dog sit there while you eat?"

Lupe grinned. "It's cute, no?"

Mark scratched Sparky's head. "Usually it's just the two of us."

An apartment to herself. The prospect of eating alone every night. She stared into the distance, watching the clock pendulum swing—back and forth—back and forth.

"You get used to it." Mark set down his fork and reached for his drinking glass. "Hadn't thought about the downside of having your own place?"

Beth shrugged. "Well—"

"Just like Chris." Mark shook his head. "Living in the moment. Your dad always gave Chris advice on planning ahead. I don't think Chris took it too seriously, but me, I took mental notes."

A phone rang in the distance. "My cell phone," Lupe said. "I'll be right back. Excuse me." She left the room.

"Living in the moment?" How dare he lecture her. He might be her elder but not by much. Not that she should let on as such. "Sounds like someone drank the Kool-Aid."

Mark furrowed his eyebrows. "Your dad's a good man."

Beth played with her food. "You're only saying that because he's old, and so are you. Old people have to stick together." If he could lecture, she could tease.

"I'm not old." Mark raised his voice.

She giggled. "Hey, whatever you have to tell yourself." Beth finished a bite of steak. A rich meaty flavor flooded her palate. Apparently, some guys could cook. None of the ones she'd dated, but this one could. Mark was full of surprises. What else would she learn about him? "This is pretty good."

"Thanks."

So much of her memory of Mark appeared to be tied to her brother. He'd been Chris's friend. Not hers. And now, she had the opportunity to get to know Mark better. Perhaps as her friend or maybe something more.

Sparky watched Mark as he finished a bite of bell pepper.

Beth stabbed another piece of steak. "You know, they finally remodeled the Hometown Café. Looks a lot different than the last time you were there."

"Really?" Mark leaned toward her. His eyes twinkled. "Tell me more."

She blinked. Mark Graham appeared to be hanging onto her every word—this was a first. She could only hope it wasn't a last.

❧◆❧

Mark finished his last bite of steak. Not that he minded chatting with Beth, but what had been keeping Lupe for so long? Perhaps she was attempting to play matchmaker and leaving them alone on purpose. It wouldn't have been the first time.

Lupe returned to the dining room. "That was my daughter on the phone. She was in an accident."

"Is she OK?" His neck muscles began to twitch, like the night he received the bad news about Chris.

"OK, but a bit scared. I need to go. I'm sorry."

"No, Lupe. It's fine. Go ahead."

It would be a shame to waste a perfectly good dinner, though. He packed up Lupe's meal and some leftovers in a plastic container. "Here. Take it with you. Glad your daughter is OK. If you need anything, call me."

Wearing a faint smile, Lupe grabbed the container. "*Gracias*, Mark. Nice meeting you, Beth. G'night."

"*Adios*." Mark waved to her as she left. He turned toward Beth. "Wanna get some coffee?" Furniture moved—check. Next on the agenda—talk about old times with Beth without prolonging his current episode. But then what?

"Sure."

Sparky jumped off his lap. Mark grabbed his plate, and Beth picked up hers. She followed him into the kitchen. As he took her dish from her, their hands brushed. Years ago, it wouldn't have meant a thing, but they weren't children anymore. Still, she was Chris's kid sister.

He decided to focus on something else— something—anything other than Beth. Trivial things were his strong suit, and what he reverted to, even in times of stress.

Mark set both plates in the dishwasher and studied the contraption. A machine that washed your dishes. A handy invention. It was crazy to think the first was designed back in 1850. Now why couldn't he think of something like that? He only needed one really good idea. Moving closer to the door, he motioned toward Beth. "Ladies first."

She walked outside, and he locked the door behind them. A yip sounded from inside, but Mark continued to wheel away from the door.

Beth followed him to his van. "Will Sparky be OK?"

Mark maneuvered up the ramp and inside his vehicle. "He was outside so much tonight, he should be OK inside for a few hours."

As he and Beth drove down Riversdale Avenue, palm trees lining the street swayed from the gentle force of a Pacific Ocean breeze. Beth rolled down her window, and the same wind flapped her highlighted locks. Mark's mind wandered, recalling their original shade. Years prior, he had moved to start a new life. Maybe Beth also changed her hair color in an attempt to move on.

Mark rubbed his left temple. Needing to pull things together before he traveled too far down memory lane and lapsed into another episode, he forced himself to focus on the situation at hand: finding a coffee shop. They could visit one of the local chains, or maybe the place over on Third. At least they had a short counter. It made life easier and more accessible. He made a right onto Third Street. If nothing else, he needed to support local businesses. It would be hypocritical if he didn't, considering how much effort and hard work it took to run his own shop.

Beth waited for him as he got out of the van. Once inside, she walked up to the counter.

Mark followed behind her. The male barista he'd seen before, on occasion, wasn't working that evening. So far, so good. Less chance of someone raising questions.

"What can I get for you?" The short, female barista asked Beth.

"I'll have a twelve ounce mint mocha, nonfat milk, no whipped cream."

"What can I get for you?" The barista stared at Mark.

He managed a slight smile. "Just coffee."

Beth stood, hands on her hips. "Just coffee? You can't go to a coffee shop and order plain coffee."

So now the little Martindale was telling him what to do? He pointed to the lettering painted on the outside window. "Read that for me."

Squinting, Beth appeared to strain to read the letters, which appeared in reverse from the inside of the window. "Surfside Coffee Shop?"

"Exactly. Coffee shop."

She rolled her eyes at him.

"I'll tell you what." He turned to the barista. "I'll have hazelnut." He grinned at Beth. "Satisfied?"

Judging from the growing smile on her face, she appeared to be.

Beth went to pay for her drink.

He put his hand up. "I got yours."

She clung to her wallet. "Are you sure?"

"I invited you. Seems only fair." Was that OK, or did that make this a date?

"Thanks, but you helped me move, and you made dinner."

"You can pick up the tab next time." Mark handed the barista a twenty then folded several singles and placed them in the tip jar. Next time. He repeated the words to himself. Maybe she didn't want there to be a next time. And yet, she didn't protest.

Beth sat at a nearby table. "Thanks again for the coffee."

Mark pushed a chair out of the way so he could move his wheelchair in place. "You're welcome."

Beth took a sip.

"So, have you found a church yet?" he asked.

"Not yet. Might visit one around the corner tomorrow. You?"

"When I go...I attend Riversdale Chapel. You're welcome to come. But I understand if it's too far for you."

Beth held her cup with both hands, stared at the lid. "I bet you're in the church choir. Probably have sung a few solos."

"Huh?"

She sipped her mocha then set it on the table and fidgeted with the lid. "Didn't you sing in school or something?"

"How'd you remember?"

Beth shrugged. "Oh, um...random memory. Figured you'd sing at your church." She removed the lid from her coffee. Her hand shook as she took another sip; coffee dribbled down one side of the cup. She swiped a napkin and quickly wiped off the spill.

Mark raised an eyebrow. "I probably should sing." He attempted to drink his coffee, but hardly any came out. Defective lids. He could see why Beth had removed hers. Mark grabbed his lid and set it off to the side.

"What's stopping you? Stage fright?"

He waved dismissively. "You wouldn't get it."

Beth propped her elbows on the table and leaned her head atop her interlaced hands. "Try me." Her inquisitive, dark eyes encouraged him to go on.

"Ever sing about God being the Great Physician, the Great Healer, when you're in a wheelchair?" He took a sip of his hazelnut coffee. Java with a subtle hint of flavor. Not bad.

"No." She lowered her voice. "But I guess it's like singing about God being your rock and shield when he allowed your brother to die."

Talk about hitting the nail on a head with a sledgehammer. An unexpected response, yet honest. Someone who understood that not everything about the Christian life was rosy. Someone who followed God when life didn't make sense. Someone with a strong faith, not the kind who believed only when things were easy. "I'm sorry about Chris."

"Sorry for?"

"Sorry for talking him into joining the Marines with me. I should have—"

"Is that what this is about? Guilt? Because I was really interested in some friendly conversation. I hope you're not doing this out of pity. You don't owe me anything."

He put up his hand atop hers. "It's not what you think. I do want to hang out and engage in"—what had she called it—"friendly conversation."

"Good." Beth smiled, revealing perfectly straight teeth no longer covered with braces. Trying to view her as the younger Martindale would be a tough task. "But try some real coffee." She handed him hers.

Hazelnut was one thing. Minty mocha, still another. He studied her cup but didn't take it.

"Don't stare at it like it's arsenic. Drink some. I promise I don't have cooties."

If Beth *did* have cooties, he sure wasn't worried about getting them.

"Mark. Good to see you out and about," said a male voice behind him.

He turned. His physical therapist stood to the side, holding two cups of coffee. What might the man say in front of Beth?

"Oscar. Good to see you, too. This is my friend, Beth."

"I'd love to chat. But I have to take this coffee home to my wife. I'll see you next Tuesday at Health Harbor." Oscar nodded good-bye and left.

"Health Harbor?" Beth asked. "The light blue building on Oleander Avenue? I think that's near my apartment."

Mark's shoulder muscles tensed. So much for relaxing. The sight of Oscar reminded him of the chair. And his reason for being in it. Not exactly a conversation he wanted to have with Beth.

"Now are you going to try that or not?" She moved her coffee closer to him.

He grabbed it and took a sip. Minty, milky, and sugary. A little sweet for his taste. "Not bad. Doesn't taste much like coffee though."

"That's the point."

"Why order coffee then?" Should he be frustrated with her or laugh? Hard to tell. The corporal in him wanted to chide her, but another part of him remembered who she was—Chris Martindale's little sister. He took a deep breath and relaxed his shoulders.

Beth grabbed her coffee, setting it in front of her. Her eyes sparkled when she looked at him. If he wasn't careful, he could get lost in her gaze.

Perhaps he needn't be in such a rush to get rid of her. Well, besides the main reason. His secrets. Although, with Beth soon to be working at Fishy

Business, he'd have to spend more time with her. If they got closer, maybe he could tell her the truth about everything, that or become adept at living a life like two different persons.

Beth smiled at him, flashing dimples near her high cheekbones. Typical Martindale feature.

Mark rubbed his neck. His shoulder muscles tensed again. Suddenly, Tim and Bill's concerns seemed well founded. He'd offered Beth a job and would keep his word. But he should limit his time with her. Hanging out with someone who reminded him of the friend he'd lost—regardless of how gorgeous or friendly she was—probably not the best idea.

6

The alarm clock blared at an intolerable level. Mark glanced toward the window. It was still dark outside. Couldn't be time to get up already. One look at the clock's display, and he groaned. Sure enough— 5:00 AM. At least he could sleep. Better than the days of reoccurring nightmares. He reset his alarm and fell fast asleep.

At eight thirty, the buzzer sounded again, and he awoke in a frenzy. He shouldn't have allowed himself to sleep in. Within fifteen minutes, he got dressed and fed the dog.

For most of his morning commute, he drove to work on autopilot but bit back a grin as he passed the Surfside Coffee Shop. There'd been some tense moments the previous evening, like when Oscar arrived. But for the most part, Mark couldn't remember the last time he'd enjoyed someone's company so much—and Beth Martindale, of all people. Even the playful teasing about his age—he didn't mind. In fact, he rather welcomed the attention.

By 9:00 AM, Mark rolled into Fishy Business.

Tim held a bag of Doritos in one hand and waved with the other. He squinted as he studied Mark's appearance then raised an eyebrow. "Nice of you to join us."

Mark gritted his teeth. Tim should feel lucky he was no longer under Mark's authority.

Bill smiled as he examined a shiny metal lure. "In ten years, you've never been late, never missed a day." He looked up from the lure and glanced at Mark.

Tim finished swallowing a bite of his chips. "Any explanations?"

Mark shrugged. "I'm getting old."

"You're only thirty-one." Bill grinned and replaced the lure in a box.

Mark shook his head. "Tell me about it. Apparently, thirty is the new eighty."

Bill's eyes widened. "College kids giving you a hard time these days?"

After finishing a yawn, Mark rubbed his eyes and held up his right index finger. "One AM. I stayed up until one." So late, and yet, time seemed to fly the night before.

"Why?" Bill asked. "Lot of papers to grade, or was there something going on at your church?"

"Beth Martindale called. She needed help moving some furniture, then we ate dinner with Lupe, and you know, talked for a while, and caught up on old times. Later on, Beth and I ended up at a coffee shop then ate dessert at an all-night diner and chatted some more." They did talk for a long time. He sighed. A real long time.

Bill cleared his throat, awakening Mark from his daydream of the night before.

"So Beth and I talked, and then I drove her home, and when I got back to my place, it was 1:00 AM. Which reminds me, you've been on my case about how we need to take inventory. Maybe we should hire someone to help us, for say, the next three weeks?"

Bill wrinkled his forehead. "Hire someone?"

Tim watched his brother inspect another lure. "To

do inventory?"

Mark nodded.

"Can't we do that?" Tim inspected his donut and took another bite.

Mark looked Tim in the eyes. "Well, I don't want to do it, do you?"

"What did you have in mind?" Tim asked.

Devising the best way to broach the subject, Mark scratched his head. "Beth starts teaching in three weeks. Until then, she has a bit of free time."

Bill stocked a box of bait in the cooler. "She wouldn't mind working at a bait store?"

Mark perceived the scent of frozen chum but didn't flinch. "Not at all." So she'd probably hate the smell. But Beth needed the money, and beggars can't be choosers.

Bill scrunched his face. "I don't know if this is a good idea. Should you two see that much of each other? What are you going to tell her...I mean, are you going to tell her about...you know what?"

"I don't know. I've been trying not to think about it. Guess I'm hoping to avoid the inevitable." Mark yawned.

Bill glanced at his brother, who stood, munching the last of his donut. "Get Corporal Graham some coffee."

"Yes, sir," Tim said, saluting the other two men.

Bill shook his head. "I can't believe you stayed up that late."

Stayed up that late or hung out with Beth? Which part was Bill having a harder time reconciling? "Yeah, me either."

Bill closed the cooler. "Good thing it's Saturday because if you had to teach, I'm not sure you'd make it."

Mark sighed. "I *am* getting old."

"What?" Bill stared at Mark, head tilted. "Why do you keep saying that? You're not old."

Mark put his head on the desk. "I feel old." He wasn't sure if the years had merely aged him or the stress of keeping things hidden.

7

The Knight looked out of county for more women in need he could help, but the prospects were slim. Up for a challenge, he would pursue a woman within Riversdale PD jurisdiction. For once, the thought of possibly being caught and indicted made his blood pulse faster. Almost as fast as the faint chugging of a locomotive in the distance.

Getting up early Monday morning, he drove to the community college. He sat on a bench in the middle of the quad and removed an object from his pants pocket. The morning sun caused the gold-colored bump key to twinkle. Now he could pick locks at Riversdale Community College. All the good ones, too. The faculty lounge. The student center. The gymnasium where the basketball team practiced—the women's basketball team—including the captain. He needed to see her.

Maybe he could convince her to stay away from the man in the wheelchair. Of course he could. Possessing an incredible power of persuasion, he'd been able to win over Juanita. For a time. Until the other man came along. And then things ended rather violently. Clearly, not the Knight's fault.

He shifted his gaze to the gymnasium in the distance. The team captain's male friend would prove to be a worthy adversary. But the Knight was aware of the rules, the standards. He had to help the girl in need, befriend her, and help her leave the man in the wheelchair. This was his challenge—his alone.

The Knight peered at his watch. Right on time. The girl entered the quad and crossed the campus for her first morning class—speech. What wonderful words might escape her crimson lips this day? If only he could get closer, go inside, listen to her.

An alarm on his watch sounded. His shoulders tensed, and he turned it off. Perhaps the timepiece might receive a blow from the hammer that evening when he was finished with it. The beeping served as a reminder that he needed to get moving.

He stole one last glimpse of the captain before walking away.

8

Beth glanced at the clock on the dashboard—8:10 AM. So much for summer vacation. Back to work. And not on time, to boot. Hopefully, her late arrival wouldn't reflect poorly on Mark. She looked in the rearview mirror and tucked a stray hair behind her ear. Given the past, working around Mark might be hard, but Beth needed the money.

While several vehicles littered the parking lot of Fan Fare, a sports bar next door, a sole black pickup sat in the parking lot of Fishy Business.

"Good morning. I'm Bill. You must be Beth." A blond man in a sci-fi t-shirt adjusted the front door sign from closed to open and shot her a grin. "Happy Monday." Bill led her to the storage area in the back of the store.

"Good morning. I'm sorry. The power in my building went out last night. I'm getting an alarm with a battery backup tonight. It won't happen again." She stared at him, awaiting further instruction. "Where would you like me to start?"

"Good question." Bill pointed to a storage area. "Over here, I guess." Boxes upon boxes of shiny metallic fishing lures and tackle lined the shelves. "We need all of this inventoried—everything you see here. These are the forms." He handed her a stack of wrinkled papers.

She examined them. "And then you want me to

transfer this information to a spreadsheet file?"

"Do you think you'll have time to do all that?"

Beth shrugged. "I don't know why I wouldn't." Mark had been kind enough to give her a job. She needed to make a better impression than she had so far. A good impression on his friends, not him, she reminded herself.

"That would make things easier." Bill began to walk away then stopped. "You know, Mark keeps track of the books by hand. Do you think you could set up something where he can do that on the computer?"

"Definitely." She could at least make work easier for the old guy. She bit back a grin. It was fun to tease Mark about his age.

Bill gave her the OK sign. "Perfect. One more thing. This is a good neighborhood, but just in case, Mark keeps a handgun in the desk drawer. Usually, I, or one of the other guys, should be here with you. But if you're here alone and for some reason you need it, well, it's there."

She wrinkled her nose at the fishy scent. That smell—what did they keep in there? Beth took a deep breath. Working with Mark, seeing his face on a daily basis, and putting up with that odor—she could do this.

An hour later, Mark and Tim arrived. A few patrons entered throughout the day. Nothing too taxing. Around noon, Bill pulled her from inventory to help wait on customers.

The doorbell chimed, and a tall, middle-aged man entered. "Hi. You work here?" he asked Beth.

She leaned her hands on the counter near the register. "Yes, may I help you?"

He smoothed his medium brown hair and pointed

to the nametag on his gray work shirt. A lopsided grin formed on his face. "I'm Randy. I restock the sodas, keep snacks on the shelves, stuff like that."

"Oh, OK."

"I didn't get your name," Randy said.

She turned and held out her hand to shake his. "Beth."

"Nice to meet you, Beth. How come I haven't seen you working here?" The goofy grin, which had subsided, quickly returned.

"I just started. I'll be working for the rest of the summer."

Randy opened the cooler. "Are you a student?"

"No, actually I'm a teacher."

"What do you teach?"

"English and drama."

"You don't say. Well, hey, I have something you might appreciate." Randy reached into his pocket and produced a cookie wrapped in a yellow plastic package. He tossed it to Beth. "Read the label."

"Sandy's *Coookies*? Whoa, one too many *O*'s."

"Yep, made by a local company." Randy chuckled. "Wonder if that *O* means there's extra oatmeal in there or something."

"Maybe." Beth suppressed a grin and began to return the cookie.

Randy gently pushed her hands away. "No, you keep it. Usually people don't get my humor. So having you working here should be fun. I'll have to show you my book of crazy misspelled signs."

"I'd like that."

Randy headed toward the door.

"Beth, can you come here for a minute?" Mark asked.

She joined Mark by the computer.

The doorbell chimed again. Randy stocked a small shelf with cookies then pointed at the packaging and shook his head.

Beth nodded. At least she'd spend some time this summer with a fellow grammarian. Maybe that would help her forget the fact she worked at a bait and tackle store.

"Hey, can you quit watching him and help me with this?" Mark pointed to his bookkeeping records.

Beth glanced at his books. "Sorry. I—"

"Is everything OK?"

"Yeah. I guess Randy is here to stock the store."

"Great. Bill said you're working on creating a spreadsheet for me. Can we discuss it?"

She stepped closer to him. "Sure."

"There are a couple of functions that would be really useful to me. If I make a list of what I need, can you set up the spreadsheet to perform those for me?"

She glanced away, attempting not to get lost in his emerald eyes. "It depends. I can make spreadsheets for a lot of different uses." And if she needed help setting things up, she could always call Dad. A benefit of having a bean counter for a father.

"I appreciate it. It would certainly make things easier around here."

Mark had helped her move and provided her with a job, not to mention he'd tried to save her brother's life. It was the least she could do. "Maybe it would allow you more free time."

Mark removed a notepad and pen from the top desk drawer. He chuckled. "Yeah? To do what?"

Had he forgotten about his mention of her paying for coffee next time? She decided to jog his memory a little. "Go to coffee shops and learn to drink something other than regular coffee."

He shook his head and pursed his lips a little, yet smiled.

Warmth flooded over her for a moment.

Mark touched her arm. "You sure you're OK?"

Attempting not to flee his warm soft touch, she turned toward him. "Other than that fishy smell in here? Yeah. And I got here late. The power was out last night, so my alarm never went off. I hate it when I wake up like that and have to get dressed in a hurry."

"No one likes to be rushed." He gave her a once over. "But for what it's worth, you look nice today."

Beth tugged at the end of her ponytail. "Nice?" She stared down at the comfy yet untrendy shoes she'd worn. Couldn't he tell she'd barely put on any makeup? Maybe his eyesight had been impaired by his time in the military. More likely he was trying to be polite.

"Thanks for trying to make me feel better." Her heartbeat skittered. Did he know her secret? Could he have remembered the note?

9

The Knight lit the tenth red candle encircling the team captain's photo and picked up an item of clothing. Carver—the name emblazoned on the back of her t-shirt—the one he'd lifted from her gym locker. Sweet Becky Carver. He set the t-shirt next to her picture, being careful not to burn the contents of the inner shrine.

He gazed at a notebook on the other end of the dining room table and allowed the sweet aroma of orange incense to pervade his nostrils. After a moment of meditation, he reached for the notebook and glanced at the notes he'd made.

7:00 AM—speech class

10:00 AM—history class

Noon—lunch in cafeteria with two members of the women's basketball team.

2:00 PM—composition class

3:00-5:00 PM—practices in gym

6:00 PM—drives homes to apartment, two blocks away; lives with roommate, who goes out of town every other weekend

Alone every other weekend. He grabbed a pen and stack of yellow paper and began to write.

Dear Becky,

How I've waited for this moment...

Not right. He crumpled the paper and grabbed a second sheet. Everything must be perfect. What if things that happened last time had been his fault? The Knight shuddered at the thought. Perhaps he'd not spent enough time explaining his plan of rescue to the previous one. He gazed at the finger-filled jar atop the entertainment center.

The Knight cradled his head in his hands. The floating finger taunted him. It'd all been his fault last time. Everything. He hadn't helped Juanita to fully appreciate the depth of his concern for her. He'd never help someone else, didn't deserve to help someone else.

"Lies!" After picking up the jar, he ran to the garage and smashed the glass into bits. Later, using gloves, he would dispose of the mess.

Perhaps that last link to the past had been holding him back. But not any longer.

10

It hardly seemed like it had been three weeks since Beth started working at Fishy Business. She studied the shelves in the storage area one last time. No more items to inventory.

Beth sneaked to the refrigerator and removed a plastic container from a paper bag. She crumpled the bag and tossed it in the trash. She took one last look at the container before closing the fridge door. Considering she'd followed her mom's directions carefully, she hoped her attempt to recreate Mrs. Graham's pistachio salad was successful.

It was time to add the final touches to the spreadsheet she created for Mark. Adjusting her hand on the mouse, she released a sigh. Maybe God caused her life to intersect with Mark again on purpose.

Tim joined her next to the computer—a bag of corn chips in one hand, a bottle of orange soda pop in the other. "We're going to miss you. Are you sure we can't keep you longer?"

She closed her spreadsheet. "Well, I do need a week to set up my classroom, but I'm sure I'll stop by from time to time. Hopefully, *after* you stock the chum for the day." It took all she had not to run from the fishy odor.

The door chimed, and Randy entered and waved.

Tim thumbed, pointing behind them, where Mark sat chatting with a customer. "Technically, he outranks us, so we don't feel as if we can make jokes about his age, but you, on the other hand." Tim winked.

She crossed her arms. "Oh, I see how it is."

"Seriously, if we teased him, we'd get the look."

"Oh, you mean the stare. Yeah, he got that from my dad."

Tim's eyes widened. "Really?"

She nodded. "I bet that look kept you guys in line when you were in the military."

"You aren't kidding."

Mark came up behind them and glared. "Still does."

His husky voice sent shockwaves through her.

"You were in the military?" Randy asked.

Mark folded his arms. "Yep. You?"

"Nope." Randy said. "Army? Navy?"

"Marine Corp." Mark wheeled closer.

"Mark served with my brother. Played football together." Beth faced Mark. "Football, baseball, basketball. What didn't you two play?"

Randy grinned. "Sounds like you've known each other a long time."

"I guess my whole life really." And yet she didn't truly know him, inside and out. Like football—Beth knew Mark played but wasn't sure what he liked best about the game.

"Mark, I have a question about this new shipment. Can you help me?" Tim asked.

Mark left with him, leaving Beth alone with Randy.

Randy set down his inventory clipboard. "Hey, I have that book I told you about."

"Thanks."

Randy held the book toward Beth. "You can

borrow it, and I can get it back from you when I stop by next week."

"That's thoughtful of you, but I won't be here. This is my last week working at Fishy Business."

"That's too bad." Randy hung his head.

Beth grabbed the book. "But that gives me another reason to stop by soon and see all my friends."

Tim and Mark joined her and Randy. "You better stop by," Tim said.

"That's right." Mark smirked. "We're all going to miss having the little Martindale around."

"Little?" Beth stepped closer to him and leaned in. "I'm not exactly ten anymore."

Mark threw up his hands in a defensive posture. "Whoa, take it easy. No one said you were."

Beth cleared her throat. "Oh yeah? Then why am I the little Martindale?"

Mark shrugged. "You're what? Five foot four?"

"Wait, my height? Oh...The little Martindale." Heat rose up her cheeks. He hadn't been teasing her about her age, or had he? Did he have any memories of her from high school, or had war injuries erased them? Only time would tell, and she wasn't sure she wanted to wait to find out.

11

"Silly girl. We could have been friends. I could have protected you from men like that." The Knight tore the basketball team captain's photo and tossed it into the flames.

Gossip spread across campus like wildfire. The girl had gotten pregnant, dropped out of college, and moved out of town. And it turned out the guy he thought was her boyfriend, wasn't after all. Still, he could have helped her. He would have been a good friend, if she would have let him. The Knight picked up a stack of newspapers from his floor. Maybe he'd burn them rather than recycle them.

Flames danced in his fireplace. Embers flickered here and there, crackling and mesmerizing him. He untied the twine that held the bundle together and removed papers one at a time and wadded them before tossing them into the fire. The page with the pictures of the teachers caught his eye—Beth Martindale. He straightened the paper and flattened it on his dining room table. Grabbing a pair of scissors, the Knight cut out her photo. With great care, he placed it in a picture frame then set it inside the circle of red candles.

Beth. Yes, she would be his next project. Spending time getting to know her shouldn't be too hard. He looked forward to learning more about her, studying her schedule, watching her every move. She'd been there, right in front of him. And based on what he'd seen, Beth might very well be in need of his assistance.

He let out a sigh and grabbed the bottle of pills off the table and took two. Needing to appear sane at work and around Beth, he'd have to take them, at least for the moment. He grabbed a pen and yellow notepad from his desk. Beth would see things from his perspective—all in due time.

12

Her third day of classes at Warner's Bay Middle School ended, and Beth hopped in her car and made the twenty-minute trek to Riversdale. She hadn't stopped by Fishy Business in days, and for some reason, she missed the place. Or was it the people—or perhaps a certain person? She entered from the back and scanned the room for him.

Mark sat at his desk, engrossed in paperwork. Tim and Bill didn't appear to be around. Mark looked up when a customer entered.

He hated being interrupted while handling the books, and she couldn't blame him. Only one way for her to handle this. "May I help you?" Beth rushed over to the elderly bespectacled customer.

"I'm looking for lures."

"This way." She led the man down an aisle. "Let me know if you need anything else."

"Thanks."

She walked over to Mark.

He looked up from his computer. "You do know I'm not paying you anymore, right?"

"I know. Just thought I'd be nice and help out—" She met his stare with one of her own. "Is there some Marine regulation against that?"

"Nope." He folded his arms. "How have you been?"

"Good. So far, I like my job. And you?"

"I really like this new spreadsheet *someone* set up for me. Saves me time."

He smiled, and warmth flooded her. Then nothing. Nope. She'd put up a wall of security, and his comment about her being the little Martindale only further cemented her fears. He'd always see her as a little girl. They could be friends, nothing more. "What are you going to do with all that free time?"

Mark scratched his chin. "Options, options. Go fishing? Spend time with Sparky? Relax and watch TV? All of the above? Do those activities meet with your approval?"

Interesting. Since when did Mark Graham consult with her before taking action? Not that she minded. "Yes… yes… and yes."

"Have you ever gone fishing?"

"Maybe once or twice with Chris and my dad."

"Sometime, you, me, and Sparky will have to take my boat out."

For no other reason than to make up for lost time with Chris? "Sounds good." She peered over his shoulder. "Be sure to click save periodically. I'd hate for you to lose your work." She reached around his shoulder to grab the mouse to click 'Save,' but ending up bumping into his hand. "Sorry." She withdrew her hand as if saving it from the clutches of a bear trap. Walls—they served a purpose. She'd placed them there for a reason, had to keep them up.

"I've made up my mind," said the customer. He plunked down three metallic lures near the register.

Beth walked behind the counter. "That'll be eighteen dollars."

The man handed her a twenty. "I've been in here for years, always the same until today. I gotta tell you.

I love the way you reorganized the lures."

"Thanks." She handed him his change.

She waved as the man left.

"Who reorganized the lures?" Mark furrowed his brows.

"I did." Was he impressed by what she'd done?

"Did Bill or Tim ask you to?"

"No, I just—"

"I had them the way they were for a reason."

"But your customer said he liked what I did."

He bit his lip. "So I heard. Thank you." A slight smile appeared on his face.

"You're welcome." Perhaps the corporal realized his way of doing things wasn't the only option.

"By the way, I wanted to thank you for the pistachio salad. At least I assume it was from you. Tasted just like my mom's recipe."

"That's because it was hers. Got it from my mom."

"It's probably my favorite dessert. Not that you'd know that. But thanks."

Not that she'd know? No, why should she? She fidgeted with her hands behind her back.

Tim and Bill entered from the back of the store.

"Hi, Beth," Tim said. "Thanks for giving the old man more time to go out. He's got a triple date with us tonight, only he doesn't know it yet."

"A date, eh?" Beth folded her arms.

"Oh, hey, you wanna come along, too?" Tim asked. "I can scrounge up another person for you. Mark, I bet your teaching assistant is not busy tonight. Why don't you call him and see if he can join us for dinner?"

They were fixing her up on a date? An uneasy feeling took hold of Beth's stomach, and it had nothing to do with the scent of chum.

Mark wheeled closer to Tim, eyebrows arched. "What?"

Beth rubbed her forehead. "Oh, don't bother. I'm...too busy. But I'm sure you'll have fun."

Mark shot her a look of understanding. "Sheesh, Tim. Leave Beth out of your scheming and matchmaking. Bad enough I have to go along with it. When did you set this up?"

"Like an hour ago. I stopped by your place. Lupe let me in, so I could grab you something decent to wear." Tim pointed to Mark's shorts. "You can't go like that."

He looked down at his outfit. "What's wrong with what I'm wearing?"

"It's fine for a hamburger joint," Bill said. "But we're going to Jack's Jetty. That nice place near the water. If I can't wear a sci-fi t-shirt and jeans, then you have to dress up, too."

Mark held up his hands. "Do I have a say in this?"

"Nope. Beth, which tie?" Tim held up a blue-gray tie and a green tie.

Choices. The blue-gray one—not very flattering. The green tie would look better on him. Then again, he'd be wearing this tie on a date with some other woman. Exactly how good did she want to help him look? Words came out of nowhere. "The blue one."

"Really?" Bill asked.

"I like the other one better." Mark pointed to the green tie.

Tim laid the green one on the counter. "She said blue."

Maybe she was messing with God's plan. Perhaps Mark was supposed to hit it off with his mystery date.

"Wait, green would look better."

"Thought you said blue?" Tim asked.

"I did, but the green..." She grabbed the tie from Tim and examined the end, then handed it back to him. "It brings out the color in his eyes." She walked toward the window. "I better go. Papers to grade." She removed a book from her bag, and her grade book fell out. "Here, can you give this to Randy?"

Tim took the book from her, and Bill handed her the grade book and a piece of paper that had slid out. "Here, you dropped this."

She examined the outside. "What is this? How did it get in my grade book? Hmmm...Addressed to Miss Martindale?"

Tim winked. "A love note from a student?"

"I sure hope not."

Mark leaned closer. "What is it?"

There was no way she was going to open it for them to read. She'd never hear the end of it. "Just some dumb note. No big deal."

Mark reached for it, but she tossed it in her bag.

"Well, I better get going," she said. Besides, you guys probably need to get ready for dinner. Have fun."

The guys waved as Beth left via the rear entrance of the store. She drove home and made herself some flavored instant coffee then sat on her couch. As she set her mug on her coffee table, a copy of her yearbook caught her eye. Beth turned to the eighth grade pictures, chuckled at her girlish ponytails and braces, and then flipped to the upperclassmen section. Mark Graham. Same wavy blond hair, same pearly white smile, same green eyes.

What happened to walls?

Maybe she didn't need them anymore. Perhaps the

reason for putting them up in the first place no longer existed.

Was there a way to test the waters without getting wet?

13

Mark finished the remaining bites of the pork chops and dirty rice he had cooked for dinner—a little bit salty, a little bit spicy—the way he liked it.

As he loaded his plate and glass into the dishwasher, Sparky hovered nearby, maybe hoping for crumbs.

Mark glanced at his calendar. September 30. School had been in session for two weeks—a logical explanation for why Beth hadn't stopped by for a while. Still, the store had grown quiet without her warm smile, her kind words, her friendship. Maybe it was better this way. He'd helped her, done his good deed. Now they could go their separate ways. Less chance of being found out. Not to mention less chance of becoming too attached. And not just for Beth's sake.

Mark had just eaten but still felt like snacking. Sparky guarded the microwave with care while his microwave popcorn cooked. A small burst of stream exited when he opened the bag. He grabbed a soda from the fridge, carried his snack to the living room, and situated his wheelchair near the couch next to Sparky.

Mark flicked through the TV channels, stopping on the History Channel. He watched for half an hour before his phone rang. "Hello?"

No one responded, only breathing on the other end. "Hello?" He'd give the jokester two more seconds before he hung up.

"Mark?" A female voice greeted him. "Hey, it's Beth."

He glanced out the window—dark outside. Maybe her car broke down, and she was stuck on the side of the road somewhere. "You OK?"

"Yeah, I'm fine. I called because I was wondering…What are you doing Saturday night?"

Mark muted the TV. "As in tomorrow? I don't know. Why? Did you buy more furniture?"

She cleared her throat. "I just found out I have to chaperone a school party."

He watched the silent screen. "Oh. That might be fun."

"You think so?" She raised her voice. "So, you'll come?"

He wrinkled his forehead. "I didn't say that." Clearly, she had misunderstood.

"You said it might be fun."

He ran his fingers through his hair. How could he explain his way out of this? "For you, for young people, but not for those of us past our prime."

"Ah, you're not that old. C'mon. I don't want to have to do this alone. Please."

Perhaps he better turn off his TV before he agreed to something else. "What's in this for me?" Besides the chance to spend time with Beth. Not that he could let on to as much.

She paused. "Free punch and chips?"

Mark looked down at Sparky, who tilted his head sideways in wonder. Sweat began to bead on Mark's brow. "Against my better judgment, I'll agree to go."

Beth squealed.

Was she excited he was going or excited she

wasn't going alone? "An entire evening spent with middle schoolers?" He sighed. "I have a feeling I'll regret this later." He regretted it already. As much as he wanted to see her, he wasn't sure he should allow himself to get closer to her.

"Thanks. You never know. You might have fun. Oh, and it's nothing formal. Khakis are fine. See you at seven thirty tomorrow."

He hung up the phone and shook his head. "Sparky, what have I done?"

જ⊷⊰ૉ

Mark grabbed a navy polo shirt and khaki pants and laid them out on his bed. Maybe too casual. He continued to rummage through his closet but stopped when he noticed his green tie—the one Beth liked. Well, or at least she thought it went well with his eyes. Who was he to argue? He placed the tie on his bed and grabbed a dress shirt and sports coat to match. After changing, he glanced at himself in the mirror, adjusting his collar. Better to be overdressed.

He glanced at his watch—7:00 PM. already. Mark headed out the door. As he drove along the center lane of the freeway, he chewed on a piece of spearmint gum and recalled the flavor was so named because of the spear-shaped, pointy leaves of the garden mint plant. But his thoughts soon drifted from history trivia to his destination.

What was he doing? Attending a middle school party—definitely not his sort of thing. Maybe years ago, but not now. But he couldn't let Beth down. The thought of the look of hurt in her innocent brown eyes made him shudder.

The sun set in the distance, only to be eclipsed by the illumination of a sea of brake lights. Traffic this late on a Friday? There must have been a fender bender.

Thirty minutes later, he arrived at Beth's building. She answered his knock wearing a navy blue dress that flared from her waist and skimmed her knees. Classy.

Beth checked out his outfit. "Great tie. I almost forgot. I'm supposed to bring some decorations. Come inside while I grab them." She scurried off to another part of her apartment.

Mark sat by her coffee table. A magazine sat on top. He caught a glimpse of an issue of the *Buckeyes* yearbook underneath. The one he'd seen earlier, the day he helped her move. He pushed the magazine aside and picked up the book to glance at the years listed on the side binding. His senior year. Hadn't Beth told him that wasn't the issue? To be fair, she probably didn't remember what year he graduated.

Small towns—twelve grades in one building and one yearbook for the whole school. So she'd made a mistake. He opened it up. Inside were signatures from various friends. He read a few of them. One he recognized. His? Odd—he didn't remember signing her yearbook. Then again, that was a long time ago, and lots of kids handed him books to sign. And what had he written?

Have a nice summer, Mark.

And a smiley face.

Wow, talk about deep. Have a nice summer. Still, it could have been worse. At least he hadn't written "Stay cool." Had Beth signed his yearbook? Did he even know where his yearbooks were? Not likely. Flipping to the underclassmen, he located Beth's photo. Nice braces. He bit back a smile in case she entered the room, not wanting to have to reveal the source of his amusement.

A closet door slammed. "Be there in a minute," Beth said. "Just need to find something."

If she organized things like her brother, it'd probably take more than a minute. He flipped to the end of the yearbook. More signatures. One caught his eye.

I see he signed your yearbook. Lucky you, Rachel.

Probably Rachel Marsh. She used to hang out with Beth. They might have even been in cheerleading together. He'd totally forgotten about that. Then again, when you play high school sports, you don't exactly pay attention to junior high cheerleaders. Intriguing. Did he have time to continue looking? It might be fun to know the identity of Beth's crush.

A door slammed at the other end of the apartment. He closed the book and replaced it under the magazine. Beth entered the living room holding five rolls of colorful streamers and a small boutonniere with a white flower.

"Is that what I think it is?" Should he have picked up a corsage? "I thought this wasn't formal."

"Relax." She set down the streamers and, boutonniere in hand, approached him. "One of my students was selling them to raise money for student council activities." As Beth leaned toward him to pin the flower to his sport coat, he detected apple-scented shampoo. Afterward, Beth planted one hand on his shoulder and appeared to study his eyes. "I didn't hurt you, did I?"

He shook his head. Mostly true. She hadn't injured him physically, but if she kept getting close like that, kept letting him in, making him think that something could exist between them, she'd inflict serious wounds to his heart.

Once outside her apartment, Beth locked the door behind her.

Mark waited for her and then wheeled toward his vehicle. "You haven't mentioned this to Bill or Tim, have you?" Though they weren't in the military anymore, he hoped still to command some sense of respect. There was nothing wrong with wanting to maintain his dignity. Since Beth arrived, Bill had done a good job of keeping Tim in line. Both had been careful not to press him about his relationship with Beth. He liked it that way. If this got out, he might have to endure some good-natured ribbing.

Beth shook her head.

"Good." He held up his index finger. "Not a word."

Beth smiled devilishly, a playful look in her eyes.

Judging from her response, all bets were off. Mark wiped the sweat from his brow. "Not a word. I mean it."

She saluted him and then entered the van.

Perhaps he should mention the yearbook and ask her about her mystery guy.

The ride to the school was much too short. Maybe another time.

Inside the school gym, Mark chatted with Beth while she put up brightly colored balloons and streamers before the party started. His teachers probably put forth the same amount of effort when he was in school. Suddenly, he appreciated them all the more.

At 8:45 PM, when the doors opened, he and Beth sat at the main table at the front of the room, near other chaperones, enjoying some fruit punch and keeping an eye on the students.

Beth played with the chain around her neck. Her hair was down but pulled back from her face. Not that his opinion mattered, but she should wear it like that more often.

He leaned toward her. "Is that a new necklace?"

She shook her head and readjusted the rhinestone pendant so it hung directly in center. "No, it just feels different."

He finished a sip of his punch. "How so?"

Beth shrugged. "It's sort of crazy, so…"

"Your necklace is crazy?" Maybe he should have let it be. Perhaps it'd been a gift from an old boyfriend, and she didn't want to drudge up the past. Given her transformation from a brace-faced teen to a beautiful young woman, she was sure to have had a few boyfriends over the years.

She turned to face him. "No, it's fine, but it feels different because normally"—Beth cleared her throat—"normally, I try to keep Chris's dog tags with me at all times. It's silly, but it makes me feel like he's close. Does that make sense?"

"It's not crazy." Mark gazed at the table centerpiece. "I keep my mom's picture in my room." He knew exactly what it felt like but hadn't been sure that anyone else did, let alone Beth Martindale.

Pop music played over the loudspeaker. Too loud and lively for his taste. Mark sighed. When would the night end?

A young Hispanic man dressed in a blue t-shirt and khakis approached their table. "Hi, I'm Antonio, the PE teacher and the football coach." He smiled and extended his hand to Beth. "You must be the new

English and drama teacher."

She shook his hand. "Yes, Beth Martindale. Nice to meet you." She gestured next to her. "This is my friend, Mark."

"Nice to meet you." Antonio nodded his head and walked away.

Beth turned toward Mark. "That was nice, introducing himself. He seems friendly."

He clenched his fists in his lap. "I'm surprised he waited this long."

"What do you mean?"

"How do I put this? That guy who stopped by— he's been looking your way all evening."

"What? Oh, c'mon. Don't start thinking every guy is staring at me. You'll end up as bad as my dad. I'll have to start calling you Jim."

Maybe it was Jim's concern, not his. But what if Mark wanted it to be his problem? He fidgeted with his collar.

Beth stared at him. "Are you...nervous?"

"Well, I don't teach here, and I'm not a student, so yes, I suppose I do feel a little out of place."

She offered him a slight grin. "I appreciate you coming."

Had he sounded like he was complaining? "So, did you ever discover the origin of your love note?"

"You mean the note in my bag? No."

"Maybe Romeo wrote it. He works here, has ample opportunity to slip a note in your bag."

Beth blushed. "Who?"

He nodded in Antonio's direction.

"Him? Nah. Probably from some student with a crush."

Speaking of crushes, he wanted to ask her about

hers. He remembered a few of the guys from Beth's class. Andy Ferrino, now there was a nice guy. Robby Jenkins, not so much. If only he had a chance to look at the yearbook again.

"I hope you're having a good time." She looked him in the eyes, furrowing her eyebrows. "So is the bait business good these days?"

"Hard to know. I seem to be finding myself spending less time at the store, more time at middle school parties." Bait business? He didn't smell like chum, did he? She certainly didn't. No, as usual, she wore the same floral fragrance he'd learned to associate with her presence. Mark leaned his head to one side, closer to his chin, still able to smell his cologne. He breathed a sigh of relief.

"Why did you come?"

Good question—Duty? Pity? Or another reason entirely—one which Mark wasn't sure he was ready to explore. He shrugged. "Nothing better to do."

"Now I know that's not true, Mr. Control Freak. Shouldn't you be making sure the store is properly stocked? Can't leave things to the fate of the other two employees. Who knows what might happen." She chuckled then traced her fingers around the top of her glass. "Is this because of Chris? Do you feel as if you need to be here because you owe him something? I thought we discussed that already."

Always so direct. They were back on the subject of Chris again. A better question might be, why had she invited him? "Maybe subconsciously? I don't know." He counted championship banners on the middle school gym walls and frowned. "That night he died, I urged him, I pleaded with him to let me talk to him about God, but then it was too late. He was dead."

Beth paled and clasped her necklace between the fingers of her right hand. "And right before he died, you tried to save him and—"

He glanced down at his legs. "Yeah." They had a relationship of some sort, and she'd earned the right to inquire. Though he hoped she wouldn't ask more.

He didn't want to be a charity case to anyone, least of all Beth. And here she was, probably worried about him because he sat in his wheelchair—the reason why their acquaintance from Beaumont, Bob Overmeyer, shouldn't have told Beth that Mark had been injured. Then again, Overmeyer could have said more but didn't.

Mark gazed at streamers and balloons off in the distance. "I don't understand why God didn't allow Chris to live. Or why I didn't die in his place. I don't even have any family left, and I lived. It doesn't really make much sense. Didn't even then." But who was he to question God?

She stretched her hand toward his, stopping short of touching him. "Chris could have accepted God. It's not your fault."

Mark set his hands in his lap and stared at Beth. The light from the ceiling reflected off her necklace, blinding him. He raised his voice to be heard over the techno tune playing. "You say that like it's so easy."

"Our parents couldn't afford to send us both to college. I got better grades, so Chris joined the military. Maybe if I had stayed at home, then he wouldn't have joined the Marines and gotten killed."

Mark scrunched his face. "That's ridiculous."

Beth's eyes widened. "Remember that the next time you think it's your fault."

Not his fault? Easy for her to say.

She bit her lip. "You know, I have this sudden urge to fish once this is over. We'd need to get some bait, but I heard there's this really good tackle store over by the lighthouse." Beth smirked.

He gave his famous stare. "Really?"

Beth grinned. "I heard the bait is good, but you have to watch out for the old, reclusive codger who runs it."

He leaned back slightly. "Old codger? Oh, you must mean Tim."

She giggled.

"Reclusive? Didn't the guys and I just go out the other evening? Right before that, I went on a couple dates with this girl from church—"

Beth nodded. "Tim told me about 'crazy cat girl.'"

Why did Tim have to open his big mouth? "So I'm old *and* single. Next subject."

"I know this nice young high school teacher. She lives in my building. I should set you up with her."

So he was good enough to date her friend. "And how many feral cats does she have?"

"Only one." She winked. "I can ask her if her cat has a list of references, if you'd like. She's a brunette. I hope that's okay. But if you prefer blondes or red heads, I can keep my eyes open. Probably eighty percent of the teachers at Warner's Bay Middle School are female, and quite a few are in my Sunday school class."

He held up his hands. "I've got nothing against brunettes." It might be fun to go out more. Then again, her friend wasn't the one he wanted to get to know better.

Students laughed in the distance. He and Beth weren't in school anymore. Five years wasn't that big of a difference, not now.

But how could he tell her that? He was ancient in her eyes, her older brother's friend. Poor guy in the chair. Nothing more. Within less than a month, Antonio would make a move. Mark was sure of it. Then his life would go back to the way it'd been before Beth showed up.

Maybe it was for the best. In the long run, he'd only end up hurting her.

14

Beth entered Fishy Business through the back. The scents of nacho cheese and chum greeted her. Wrinkling her nose, she attempted to block out the fishy smell.

Tim spotted her first. "Long time, no see."

If Chris were still alive, she would have approached him with her problem. Of late, Mark had assumed the protector role in her life. By his own choosing or because of guilt, she wasn't sure. Beth glanced around the store. No sign of him. Her heart sunk. "Is Mark here? May I speak with him?"

"He should be here in a few minutes. Reaching into the cooler, Tim grabbed a can. "You want a soda while you wait?"

Beth waved dismissively. "Nah. Thanks though. I'll wait for him out back."

Beth sat at a picnic table then retrieved her MP3 player from her bag. No sense just sitting there while she waited. She hummed and tapped her foot to the beat of a lively Broadway musical soundtrack.

A hand grasped her shoulder. She jumped, then paused her MP3 player.

"Sorry, didn't mean to scare you." Mark's husky voice soothed her.

Beth removed her earphones.

Mark raised an eyebrow. "Classical? Country? Rock?"

"It's a song from a musical."

Mark folded his arms in his lap. "Tim said you wanted to talk to me?"

"Something happened at school. Probably nothing. A little weird, that's all."

"You OK?"

Beth unfolded the yellow paper. "I got this note. Probably some kid trying to be funny."

Arching his brow, Mark cast a parental look. "Another one?"

She shrugged.

"How many have you received?"

Beth hung her head.

He tipped her chin toward him. "How many, Beth?"

She willed herself not to make eye contact with him. "Six."

"Six? Here, give me that." He swiped the note from her.

"'I'm your one true friend. I'll keep you safe and protect you. You don't have to be afraid of me. You belong with me. You'll see. I'll prove it to you. Your White Knight.' White Knight? Did your class read medieval stories recently?"

Beth shook her head. She'd assumed a student had written it, but what about an adult? Antonio had been rather friendly lately. His eyes often met hers when they crossed paths in the halls or the teacher's lounge. Teachers had access to each other's contact information for emergencies, which meant he knew where she lived. She'd better not tell Mark. He'd overreact.

Beth peeked over Mark's shoulder as he reread the note. "Probably some kid being stupid, right?"

He examined both sides of the paper. "Joke or not,

kids shouldn't be sending you this stuff. It might be harmless, but I don't like the possessive tone of this note. Where did you find this?"

She snatched back the note. "On my desk at the end of the day, like the others. Well, other than the one I found in my bag."

"Have you shown this to anyone else?"

"No. I wanted to show you first. I knew…" Her eyes met his concerned stare. "I knew you'd know what to do."

"First thing tomorrow, take it to the principal's office. If he doesn't listen, I'd talk to a union rep. Promise me you'll tell someone." He rested a hand on her forearm.

"Yeah, I will."

Mark gave his famous stare then shifted his gaze to her arm and slowly released his hold.

"I promise. By the way, next Saturday, I'm setting you up with my friend Marisa. You could take her out for a nice dinner or go to the movies."

"Anything else I need to know or do?"

"I'm only trying to help."

He furrowed his brow. "I'm not exactly Brad Pitt. What did you tell this poor girl?"

Maybe not Pitt but still good looking. Not that he'd believe her if she told him. "Sheesh. Quit acting like you're dead."

Mark released a sigh and muttered. "Quit acting like I'm a whole man."

Her heart sank. Did he think that because of the wheelchair? She'd never seen him as anything less. "Mark, I didn't mean—"

He put up his hand. "It's OK. A moment of self-pity. This girl lives in your building, right?"

"Yeah."

"Saturday at 1800 hours...uh, 6:00 PM. I'll stop by your apartment complex."

"You sure?"

He nodded.

She shouldn't have pushed him so much. Maybe he didn't want her help. And why such the urge to help him find someone else? Perhaps it was easier than dealing with past emotions.

15

Beth marched next door to visit Marisa. After disappearing for a minute, Marisa walked out of her kitchen holding two coffee mugs—white with cats on the side—and set them on her cherry coffee table. Her friend brushed her short, wispy dark brown hair out of her face before taking a sip of her coffee. "Sorry I couldn't go with you to the back-to-school party, but at least I'm over the flu."

"It's OK. I roped my *friend* Mark into going with me." The word rolled out of her mouth and set her on edge. How else would she describe him?

"Your friend from home?"

Beth nodded. "He's nice, but he seems sort of lonely. I should set him up with someone from church." Beth sipped her coffee, burning her tongue in the process.

Marisa leaned forward. "Like who?"

Beth set her cat mug on the coffee table. So Marisa liked felines. She wasn't housing fifty in her apartment. Animal control wasn't beating down her door. Besides, Mark had already dated at least one girl that was head-over-heels about cats, and he'd admitted he was pro-brunette. Beth bit back a grin and gave Marisa a wide-eyed stare.

Marisa pointed to herself. "Me?" Her jaw dropped.

Beth had hoped for a better response. "Marisa,

c'mon. You should have dinner with him. He's nice, funny, smart, knows a lot about history. Not to mention, he's good looking."

Marisa sipped her coffee and stared out her living room window. "If he's so great, why don't you date him?"

Beth folded her arms. It had nothing to do with the wheelchair. Her grandpa had been in one, and he still got around and lived his life just fine. What was it then? Eighth grade. Nope, don't bring it up. Let it go. "Mark? He's like a brother to me."

"Well, you do a lot of things together."

Beth shrugged. "Yeah, so?" Her stomach tightened, and nervous laughter escaped her lips. "Since when did it become a capital offense to befriend someone of the opposite sex?"

"I guess I figured there was more between you two than being just friends."

"We hang out a little, but I assure you, we're only *friends*. Nothing more." That word again. It mocked her.

"I don't know, Beth. I need to work on ideas for the yearbook. I don't have time to go out right now."

"I have plenty of old yearbooks in my apartment. You could borrow some. Go out. Have fun." Somehow screaming "Help me keep my distance from him" was out of the question.

Marisa walked toward the kitchen. "That's nice, but I don't even know him."

Nice—was there a faint glimmer of hope? Time to move in for the kill. Beth picked up her mug and followed Marisa. "I told him I'd try to get him a dinner date for tonight." Sure she should have asked sooner, but that would have given Marisa more time to invent excuses.

"Tonight?" Marisa furrowed her brow. "Hey, that's your problem. If you want me to get to know him, maybe bring him to church some Sunday so I can meet him, OK?"

"All right. Have it your way."

Now what?

16

Three times the Knight ran his hands under the water. He could stop washing now.

After turning off the bathroom light and checking it twice, he made his way down the hall. The faint aroma of orange incense that traveled down the hallway tickled his senses.

The obsessive behavior—he could never win Beth over, not like this. He had to attend a support group. That was his only chance of a semi-normal existence.

Everything needed to be perfect—just like her. Maybe that's why his plans had failed before—because they had been anything but perfection.

Still, things were looking up. The Knight had improved.

He'd been working steadily and getting out of the house more often. That was how he'd run into Beth in the first place. The way her dark eyes twinkled and her warm smile glistened...when she looked at Mark and not him. He slammed his fist against the wall.

Problem was, when the Knight came home, that's when things set in.

After spending all day interacting with others, he became keenly aware and had time to obsess.

The act of smashing the jar from atop the entertainment center had done something to him. He'd searched the attic for Juanita's picture. Why *did* he still keep a photo of her? No matter. Nothing Beth needed to know about. He could still be her friend.

He removed a yellow notepad from his desk and sat down to write. Only writing allowed him to express his inner feelings.

There was no other way he could tell Beth how he felt. At least not for now. Maybe in time he could get her alone and let her know how much he cared.

17

Beth dragged herself back to her apartment and slumped onto her couch. She turned on the TV but muted the volume. The world was silent yet deafening.

She and Mark did spend a bit of time together. And what frightened her the most—she enjoyed every last minute.

Beth glanced at the mantel clock atop her end table—4:15 PM. However well meaning, she wished she hadn't concocted her plan. She picked up a yearbook, flipped open to the first page of signatures. Thoughts of pep rallies brought a smile to her face, and just that quickly, misunderstandings from eighth grade pervaded her thinking. She slammed the yearbook shut.

No matter what happened in the past, she couldn't cancel over the phone. That would be rude. She trudged outside to her car and drove away.

Hardly a cloud was in sight when she pulled into the parking lot of Fishy Business. Tim and Bill stood inside.

"Is Mark here?" she asked.

"No, sorry, Beth. Tim and I helped Mark take his boat near the lighthouse. A friend lets him use their dock. He might be able to get cell reception out there. You could try giving him a call. I ... uh..." Bill blushed. "I assume you have his number."

"I'd rather speak to him in person."

"Do you know how to get to the Del Mar Lighthouse?"

She shook her head.

"Tim, can you give her directions?"

Tim opened the desk drawer and removed a yellow memo pad and pen.

After several attempts to scribble on the paper, he tossed the pen in the trash. "This pen's out of ink. I'll print them for you. Probably neater than my handwriting anyway."

Bill leaned against the wall. "Mark said you received a strange note again?"

Tim shot her a look of concern.

"The principal is handling it. No need to worry."

Tim printed the directions and handed them to her.

"Thanks." She hurried out the door. Would Mark feel rejected when she told him? Maybe she could go with him instead, to make up for his missing date. But what if he thought she'd set things up like this on purpose?

❧

After parking near Riversdale Beach, Beth paced toward the lighthouse entrance. A seagull hovered overhead and cawed. Startled, Beth jumped then relaxed, releasing a sigh and inhaling salty marine air, her hair unfurling in the ocean breeze.

Following the lighthouse path, she debated her reason for not telling Marisa about the date sooner. Marisa would have used the time to concoct excuses. Or, maybe Beth wanted Marisa to say no in the first place. That would mean—she shook her head—

thoughts she didn't want to consider. Feelings that went back as far as junior high.

Mark's rolled-up sleeves revealed an upper body in shape as good as, if not better than, when he'd played football in high school. Beth studied the brown, basket-woven tackle box resting open on his lap. She retrieved a photo from her pocket and handed it to him. "It's a picture of us. From the back-to-school party. I have doubles, so you can keep it."

"Thanks." Mark smiled as he looked at the photo then wedged it inside a book in his tackle box. He held up a metallic lure with red and yellow feathers dangling from the end and examined it. "According to my watch, dinner is not until 1800 hours, so I still have some time left. Wanted to get a little fishing in beforehand."

Beth stood near where he sat, hands clasped behind her back. "I'm sorry, but Marisa can't make it tonight. I wanted to find you before you drove over to my apartment complex."

"Oh well."

She bit back a grin. "Don't sound so disappointed."

"I'm guessing my photo scared her away." Mark winked.

"No, I didn't show her the photo. It's my fault. I'm not the most organized person, and I waited 'til the last minute to ask her. She had to work on the school yearbook. Besides, she's really young, and I'm sure you like older women." She managed a lopsided grin. "You know, ones who are more"—she fingered her dangle earrings—"quiet and who knit."

He chuckled. "Knit? Might I remind you I'm not eighty?"

Good. She'd made him laugh. "Don't worry. I'll help you find someone."

"Great. Thanks, Miss Matchmaker. In the meantime, would you care to check out the lighthouse?"

"Sure." The lighthouse stood maybe two hundred feet high. White with black at the top. As beautiful as her brother had described in his letters. And here she was, finally standing next to it, and with Mark Graham by her side. Wonderful and unnerving at the same time.

They continued toward the lighthouse and stopped on the sidewalk for a moment to take in the majestic view. Waves crashed back and forth, occasionally interrupted by the sound of seagulls above. A vast number of crags scattered below formed part of the network of rocks lining the shore.

Beth stared off in the horizon. "It's beautiful…and so peaceful."

Mark nodded. "Built in 1912 by a Spanish architect."

After a few minutes, Beth removed her sandals and walked on the beach.

Mark wheeled across the sand. Special, larger wheels were fastened to his chair. They must have helped him gain traction.

Beth glanced down at the innumerable grains of sand. "God's promise to Abraham about his descendants. It makes sense. I guess you have to encounter sand to understand the promise."

"I hadn't given it much thought before, but you're right on target."

"Guess it was as hard for someone like Abraham to trust God. Sure, people in the Bible had more physical encounters with God, like the burning bush and whatnot, but think about trusting God to fulfill a promise after you're dead and gone."

Mark stared at her.

Had she done something wrong? "What?"

He shrugged. "Just listening. I didn't expect you to carry on such weighty discourse. Not that it's bad. I haven't had too many serious conversations involving God lately. I don't go to Bible study as much as I used to. To hear you talking about God, it ignites a little passion inside. One I've brushed aside for a while. Perhaps out of fear." Mark watched the waves for a moment. "I love God," he leaned on his armrests and hung his head, "but sometimes, it's hard to trust the Good General. Completely irrational, right?"

"When Chris died, my dad told me God loved Chris more than we did, so we had to trust God knew what he was doing. I don't always understand God, but I know I need to trust Him." She fidgeted with the dog tags that hung around her neck. "That said, it's not always easy."

A minute later, Mark rolled forward. "I'm going fishing. Care to join me?"

"Sure, why not." The summer sun further dried Beth's already chapped lips. She reached into her pocket and moistened her mouth with cherry lip balm. Mark stared at her. "Sorry. They were chapped."

"I'll take your word on that."

Heat rose in her cheeks, and she quickly slipped the lip balm back in her pocket and pushed her sunglasses further up her nose, hiding behind them as much as possible.

They headed farther along the beach, down to the dock—six hundred feet of weathered two by fours—to where his boat was tethered. "I'd advise you to put your shoes back on before walking on the dock. I can't guarantee there won't be any splinters."

A dog yipped. Beth spotted Sparky on board the small fishing pontoon. The black creature sported a bright yellow life jacket. Beth smirked. What a funny little animal.

Mark rolled along the dock and onto the pontoon boat, using a wheelchair accessible ramp. He held up a life jacket and handed it to her. "Safety first. Everyone wears a jacket on my boat, even the barge dog." He looked at the animal. "Isn't that right, Sparky?"

Beth saluted Mark. "Aye, aye, captain." She slipped on her life jacket while Mark fastened his. "So why are they called barge dogs?"

"They make great ratters onboard barges, not to mention they're good guard dogs."

She nodded. "Oh. I see. With such large teeth, not a surprise. Wow, good at guarding and delivering messages."

Mark glanced at her sideways.

Yes, she'd remembered other facts he'd spouted. Did that surprise him? "What? Occasionally, I listen."

The closer she got to the boat, the worse the odor of bait. That is, until Mark reached to help her onboard. The masculine, outdoorsy scent of his cologne provided a fresh relief from the fishy smell. A round, white life preserver sported the name of the peach-colored pontoon in black lettering—*Orange Roughy*.

She took a seat on the end of the pontoon, away from the khaki overhead canopy that covered the rest of the boat. She removed a ponytail holder from her pocket and tied back her hair. "How far are we going?"

"Far enough out so we can fish." Mark secured his

chair nearby and headed the boat away from shore.

"So, *Orange Roughy*? Did you come up with the name yourself?"

"For the boat? Yeah."

So he'd named the store and the boat. Interesting. "Nice."

Perfect weather. Cute dog. Nice guy. Relaxing boat ride. Nothing to do but fish. And what exactly was the downside?

࿎ঌ

The glimmer of the sunset reflected off the ocean. Relatively calm seas. Mark figured he should enjoy the moment. Yet something nagged at him. Why bother to set up a date for him with her friend but still spend so much time with him? Beth couldn't be interested in him. Maybe she needed another job.

He grabbed a couple of sodas from the cooler and handed one to Beth. "Thanks."

"You're welcome." He opened his can, took a sip. "So what happened with the strange note you received?"

"The principal is looking into it. No new notes, so I feel better." Sparky jumped on Beth and sniffed the outside of her can. She petted the dog on the head.

"Are you planning on going home for Thanksgiving?"

A gull sounded overhead. Sparky ran to the other end of the boat, jumped on a seat, and yipped.

"I don't know yet. Haven't thought that far ahead. You know me, living in the moment."

Ouch. So she *did* occasionally listen and still remembered his comment. Maybe he'd been too harsh.

"By the way, I wanted to tell you. My parents said Mr. Crandy bought your old house and added a second story."

"Oh." He imagined what the exterior would look like. Maybe he should go home sometime to see it. Then again, it didn't matter. It wasn't like it was his house anymore.

"My folks have always liked you. Thought you were a good friend to Chris. And you were."

Yeah. Some friend. He couldn't even save him. Mark baited his hook and cast his rod. Then he baited a second and handed it to Beth. Their fingers brushed in the exchange. Despite the heat of the summer sun, her hands were cold. Maybe he should rub some warmth into them.

"Thanks."

He reeled his line in a little. "Once you asked me if I hung out with you because of guilt. So I ask you, why do you spend time with me?"

"What do you mean?"

"You could be hanging out with friends who could run and play volleyball on the beach, or something like that."

Beth's eyes widened. She put one hand to her chest and gasped. "Oh, my goodness. You're in a wheelchair. I hadn't noticed."

Drama Queen. Mark shook his head and tried to suppress a smile at her sarcasm. Finally, he'd found a girl who didn't care about his condition, yet he couldn't be honest with her. No matter what Beth thought, he wasn't a whole man.

She furrowed her brow. "You plan on growing a third eye or horns?"

"No." Hard not to chuckle at that.

"Well then…On the other hand, a third arm might actually be useful for fishing."

So she wanted to spend time with him, no strings attached. Too good to be true.

When would the other shoe drop?

৵৽

Beth hunched forward and gripped her rod between her hands. "I've caught something."

Mark leaned toward her. "You got it?"

"Think so." After a few minutes of playing tug of war with the creature, she reeled in an odd-looking fish. Yellowish tan with orange, black, and brown spots on the top and sides and white on the bottom.

A look of pride spread on Mark's face. He inspected the fish and placed it in a container. "Looks like a thirteen-inch spotted bay bass." He patted her on the shoulder. "Not bad."

She smiled inside. Too bad Chris or her dad weren't around to see her big catch.

"Not bad at all." He winked. "For a girl."

She scowled and squinted at him as he grabbed her rod.

Beth snatched the rod from him. "I can do it." She smirked. "I wouldn't want the old guy to hurt himself." She attempted to bait her hook, but her finger became caught. "Ow. I hooked myself. It's bleeding." So much for attempting to act tough.

"Let me see. Hold still." Mark reached for her hand and examined her fingers. "Give me a minute." He found his first aid kit, stashed near his chair, and patched her up with a tube of antibiotic ointment and a Band-Aid. "Here, good as…" He looked up. Their eyes met and locked in a tender moment.

Warmth flooded over her. He had a gentle touch. Something safe and comforting about him. More than friends? Maybe Marisa had been right after all. Beth cleared her throat and glanced at her watch. "You know, I should go home soon. It's getting late."

"We haven't been fishing that long. Is something wrong?"

What was she doing there with him? Eighth grade. The school play. Pep rallies all over again. Was her head spinning? It sure felt like it. She shrugged. "No. Well, yes. I…" Her yearbook. Were they more than friends? "Just remembered something Marisa said." That was true. "I better go help her with the yearbook layout."

"OK, we'll go back." Mark turned the boat around. They sat in silence as they made their way back to the shore, and Mark docked the boat. "Do you need to help your friend right this minute?" he asked. "Perhaps you can call her?"

That word again. *Friend.* If she and Mark were just *friends*, why did this whole exchange seem awkward, uncomfortable even? Was that hurt in his eyes? Beth averted her gaze and sighed. The one time she wished she was truly invisible to Mark. "It's better if I go now. Sorry."

Sparky yipped and followed her as she left.

"C'mon Sparky. Leave her be."

The dog turned on his heels and scurried back to his master.

Beth jogged to her car. In her hurry, she fumbled for her keys then started the ignition. Why was she suddenly clumsy, with legs like a middle schooler? She reached the freeway and drove toward her apartment—a ride that suddenly seemed longer than before.

ॐॐ

Mark spied a rock formation in the distance and wheeled toward it. The waves crashed, over and over again, like the thoughts tumbling through his mind. Why didn't she remember her obligation to help her friend earlier? Then again, she was quite the free spirit, forgetting to charge her cell phone. He had tried to be gentle, tried not to hurt her taking out the hook.

Or maybe she had other plans—better than fishing with a guy in a wheelchair. Like plans with a male teacher.

And what about Tim? He was the first to lay eyes on Beth when she'd been stranded in their parking lot. Could his friend have stooped so low as to divulge Mark's secrets? If so, maybe Beth warned Marisa to stay away. Maybe Beth came to confront Mark but then lost her nerve and backed down at the last minute.

He dropped off Sparky then drove to Fishy Business. On the way there, he changed the radio station three times. No matter how hard he tried, every song reminded him of Beth. Fourth time might be the charm.

The old love song about what a man would do when he loved a woman played over the radio waves as he pulled into the front parking lot of Fishy Business—the spot where Beth had first parked— where they'd run into each other. He went inside and grabbed a soda from the cooler. The same beverage he'd taken to her while he helped her with her tire. Too many reminders.

The register drawer slammed shut and caught his attention.

Bill counted change to a customer then waved to the man as he left. He faced Mark. "Back so early? How was dinner?"

"Huh?" Mark made momentary eye contact. "It's a long story. Beth's friend was busy, so Beth and I took the boat out for a while." He could talk about it to try to gain answers, but opening up about his relationship with Beth might only expose him to teasing.

Sighing, Mark opened his can and took a huge gulp.

"Anything you want to"—Tim cleared his throat—"uh, talk about?" He opened yet another bag of chips.

Mark could ask the same question. Perhaps there was something Tim wanted to share. "We went out on the boat, she caught a fish—big one too, and later, she hooked her finger, and then…" He shook his head.

Tim smirked. "You didn't get all professorial and recount tales of the discovery of Band-Aids, did you? Or tell her about the history of the use of leeches for medicinal purposes, or—"

"No. None of that. I tried to help her, and she said she wanted to leave." Rather quickly too.

Bill closed the register drawer. "You seem bothered by that."

"She left so abruptly. I hope I didn't do or say something to hurt her." The last thing he wanted to do was to hurt the Martindales—any of them.

"Well, sometimes, you appear menacing." Tim nodded as he munched.

Bill glared at his brother then stared at Mark. "So do you like her or what?"

Mark shrugged. "We have fun together. She's a

good friend."

Tim smiled. "You're from the same area. That's kind of cool."

Cool and awkward at the same time. "It feels a little weird. I was best friends with Chris." Besides, what would she want with a guy like him, one with such scars? Assuming Tim hadn't already said anything, and Mark and Beth got closer, he'd have to tell her everything.

"And that's a problem because...?" Bill asked.

"Because I was there when Chris died."

"Yes, you were. But so was I and so was Tim and the rest of our unit."

"Yeah, I'm not afraid to ask her out," Tim said.

Mark clenched his teeth. Maybe Tim did have a thing for Beth.

Tim patted him on the shoulder. "I'm kidding. Look, before you ran into her, you couldn't talk much about Chris's death. I think she's good for you."

Mark nodded. Maybe he shouldn't have doubted his friend. "You're right. She did help me to talk about Chris's death more."

"You're going to tell her everything eventually?"

"Wasn't planning on it. Guess I need to. I'm afraid of what she'll think. In fact, even talking about telling her is stressful."

"You seem to enjoy each other's company," Bill said. "Maybe opening up to her might help. Beth seems understanding and compassionate. The longer you wait to tell her, the worse it'll be. Anyway, let's just say we're thinking of making you a silent partner because you spend so much time away from the store."

Tim sighed. "Women are complicated."

Mark shook his head. "Tell me about it. I'd like to

know what happened tonight, but maybe I should let it go unless she brings it up." The way she hung out at the store, he'd run into her soon. As much as girls liked to talk, she was bound to let something slip about the incident.

"That sounds like a good idea," Bill said.

Mark stared at Bill. "Why is it that in some ways being in the Corps seems better than civilian life? Think about it. There's always proper chain-of-command, standard operating procedures, a sense of order about things." He sighed, heading for home.

Too bad SOPs didn't exist for women.

Once home, he wheeled to the back door and let Sparky outside. The ride home had been a blur. Having traveled on autopilot, he thanked the Lord he hadn't wrecked his car.

He sat at the dinner table alone and stared into the distance, unsure of what he felt for Beth. First, his friends thought he should avoid Beth, and now Bill told him honesty might be helpful.

If he told Beth everything, she might get mad at him or never forgive him. Getting close to Beth while keeping secrets was like playing with fire. Someone was bound to get burned.

18

The late afternoon sun shone through Beth's windshield as she sat in the Warner's Bay Middle School parking lot. She cranked the engine. Nothing. She checked her fuel gauge, but the needle indicated her tank wasn't empty. Beth had stayed late to chaperone and lead the monthly drama club meeting and then to meet with a parent, who later called and cancelled. By now, most other teachers, including the bubbly female math teacher across the hall, had left for the day. A little unnerved at the thought of being stranded in the school parking lot alone, Beth reminded herself the notes from the Knight had stopped. But why? Had the Knight become scared and stopped writing, or was he lurking in the shadows, watching her every move and calculating his next step, waiting for the opportune time to encounter her alone—like now.

"Everything OK?" a male voice asked.

She gasped and looked up from the dashboard. Only Antonio, the PE teacher.

He flashed a smile. "Car trouble? I'd be more than happy to help."

She didn't want to call Mark. But neither was she sure she wanted to accept help from Antonio. "My car won't start."

Antonio glanced at her dashboard. "Well, it's not your battery." He propped open the hood and looked inside. With each passing minute, Beth's mental cash register raised the total on her car damage. Something she hadn't budgeted for. She'd need to look for a second job—something she'd been wanting to do anyway to prove to Mark and her dad that even the littlest Martindale could be responsible and take care of herself.

Antonio closed the hood.

"How bad is it?"

"Could be the fuel pump, but I don't have the tools I need to look at it here. I can call a friend of mine, and he can tow it back to his garage. I'll make sure he gives you a good deal." Antonio smiled.

"Thanks." As much as Beth wished to avoid awkwardness between her and Mark, right now, she longed for his presence. Though there was definite history between them, that familiarity was part of what helped her to feel safe. While she knew plenty—good or bad—about Mark, she was unfamiliar with Antonio. Still, she couldn't continue to run to Mark whenever she encountered trouble.

When the mechanic arrived, Beth let Antonio and his friend do most of the talking.

The mechanic closed the hood and wiped his hands on a rag hanging from his pocket and faced Beth. "I'm going to need to keep it at least overnight. Do you have a ride home?"

"I'll give her a ride," Antonio said. "Thanks, man. Call me when it's ready." Antonio waved to his friend, and he and Beth got in his car. "I don't know how long it will take him to get the right parts and get it fixed. Don't worry though. I can give you a ride to work until your car is fixed."

"Are you sure? You don't need to do that."

"That's what friends are for."

Right now, with plans that included avoiding Mark, Beth could use a friend. If nothing more, someone to share her concerns about the Knight.

She glanced out the window. As much as she wanted to tell Antonio about the notes from the Knight, fear prevented her. If he wasn't the Knight, he might think less of her as a professional for being afraid of a silly message from a student. If he was the Knight, it would be better not to discuss the communication.

She studied him as he drove. He could be the Knight. But then so could anyone. All someone would have to do is find a less-than-scrupulous janitor and offer him some money in exchange for access to her classroom or be adept at picking locks. Or be a teacher. Antonio could easily ask the janitor to unlock her room. Her shoulders tensed. Or maybe the janitor himself.

"Everything OK?"

"Yeah. It's been a long day."

Antonio paused at the light. "Which way to your place?"

"Oh, sorry." She gulped then reminded herself that as a teacher he already had access to her address. "Make a right here."

Minutes later, they arrived in front of her apartment. "Thanks for the ride."

"You're new. And while the school is in a safe neighborhood, you don't want to sit there stranded. I moved here a couple of years ago, and it's tough when you're new and trying to make friends. And with the problems you're having with your car, you seem like you could use some help."

That was it—friendly help with no strings attached? "Well, I appreciate all you've done."

"I can stop by tomorrow morning to pick you up. Is six thirty OK?" Other options had to exist, and yet she couldn't think of any. Marisa came to mind. But with her high school schedule being different from Beth's, carpooling wasn't an option.

"Yes, thanks again." Beth hopped out of the vehicle.

Antonio waved and drove away.

Once he was gone, thoughts about the Knight still raced through her mind. She checked every square inch of her apartment before going to bed. With each passing hour, she remained awake, the red glow of her alarm clock taunting her.

19

Beth gazed out the window as Antonio drove along Riversdale Boulevard. The bank marquee on the corner alternately displayed the time, date, and temperature. The date stuck in her mind. Two weeks had passed since she last saw Mark.

A sign on the side of the road indicated only two more miles to the mall. Beth grasped her purse. She might be low on cash, but she could still window shop.

While stopped at an intersection, Antonio turned up the volume on his radio and stared at the red light. "I'm thirsty. Can we get something to drink? A soda maybe?"

At this rate, they were never going to get to the mall. She questioned whether he really needed a soft drink. On the other hand, when her car had given her problems last week, he'd been more than willing to help her. And until hers came back from the mechanic, she would need to rely on him for a ride to and from work.

Beth flipped down her mirror and adjusted her hair. "We're almost at the mall. You could get something at the food court."

"I'm pretty thirsty, and I'd sort of like to find a bathroom, too. Wait, there's a place. It'll have to do."

She flipped back the mirror.

Antonio pulled his blue truck into the front parking lot of Fishy Business.

Her shoulders tensed. "Why here?"

"I bet they have a restroom and maybe something to drink."

Right on both accounts.

Antonio got out of the car, door still open. "You're not coming inside?"

"No, thanks."

"Come on. Don't sit here by yourself."

"I…" How sad was it that a drama teacher couldn't act her way out of this? "OK." With any luck, Mark wasn't working today. It felt odd coming in the front entrance. She kept her sunglasses on and ignored the door chime announcing their presence.

"I'll be right back." Antonio walked toward the right.

But the restroom was on the other side. *Go left.*

He must have spotted the sign because he headed the other way.

How fast could she get his drink and leave? She hoped Antonio wouldn't put up a fight like Mark. Mark would fuss about a woman buying him something. Not that it was a bad trait in him, but at the moment, she needed to speed things up and get out of there.

Beth grabbed a soda and strolled to the counter where Tim worked the register.

"That'll be a dollar fifty, ma'am."

She handed him a five-dollar bill. If she kept a low profile, maybe no one would recognize her.

Tim glanced at her for a minute. "Beth?"

Busted. "Hi, Tim."

He turned around, "Hey, Mark, look who's here."

Antonio walked back from the restroom, and Beth handed him his drink.

Mark looked at them from behind his desk but said nothing.

She wished a massive earthquake would open up the ground and swallow her whole. "Hey, Mark, Antonio. You might remember each other from the back-to-school party." Did Mark wonder why she'd stopped coming around?

Antonio leaned over and whispered, "Shouldn't we be going to the mall?"

Before she could respond, he touched her shoulder.

Had Mark seen? And why did she care? Beth could explain that she and Antonio were just friends, but it wasn't like Mark deserved an explanation. Except for maybe because he'd suggested Antonio had an interest in her. But it wasn't like that.

"Sorry, but we really have to go. See you later." She waved and jetted out with Antonio.

The vending truck sat in the driveway. Randy entered the store as Beth and Antonio left. Randy waved. Maybe she should have stayed longer and chatted with everyone.

Antonio turned toward her. "Everything OK with you?" She managed a slight smile. "Yeah." The sick feeling in the pit of her stomach begged to differ.

20

Friday afternoon, Beth entered a student's grade into the online progress report program on her classroom computer then gathered up her belongings. Wow. Four thirty already? If she didn't leave now, she'd be there all night.

The security guard had escorted her outside the previous month, but the notes from the Knight had stopped. No sense in bothering the guard now.

Beth flipped the light switch and stepped outside her classroom. She caught the shadow of a man's frame from the corner of her eye. Maybe the Knight! She jumped and shrieked, her heart racing.

Antonio threw up his hands. "It's just me." He placed one hand on her shoulder. "You OK?"

She clutched one hand to her chest. "Sorry. I wasn't expecting you to be standing there."

He walked down the hall beside her. "Hey, I don't have a game tonight. Would you like to see a movie?"

"It might be fun." She smiled and strolled along with him, passing brightly colored bulletin boards along the way. Cheerleaders chanted in the gym at the end of the hall. Kids were having fun, so why couldn't she? The voice of reason interrupted her thoughts. "I'd love to, but I have to grade a few more papers, and then I need to go to the mall. But after that, I'm free."

"Cool. There's this new action-adventure movie I want to see. You up for it?"

"Sure." Beth walked with Antonio to the parking lot. Further proof she no longer needed the security guard to follow her outside. Besides, it seemed the kid who'd written the notes had gotten the message.

When they reached her car, Antonio's phone rang. He looked down at the display and sighed. "It's Coach Saunders. I have to take this. See you tonight."

Beth waved and then drove away. She doubted she could be any more exhausted than she already was. Still, Antonio had been a good friend, so she could at least hang out with him a little.

She'd barely finished grading homework assignments when Antonio called. Minutes later, he met her at her apartment and drove them to the mall.

As wind rattled leaves on the trees surrounding the mall parking lot, Beth was glad she'd decided to pull her hair back. She entered the building with one goal in mind: find a second source of income, preferably one that didn't require her to have to interact with Mark. After a quick stop at the drinking fountain, she toured the mall with Antonio, noted the stores with "Help Wanted" signs, and decided on her plan of attack. On her way out of California Chic, Beth added another application to the stack in her purse as she passed several well-dressed mannequins. She'd successfully moved all her junk to Riversdale and almost secured not only one but two jobs. A feeling of pride swept over her.

Antonio sat on a wooden bench in the center aisle of the mall, next to a planter of red and pink geraniums. His warm smile greeted her. "Got what you needed?"

She nodded. The extra money would help her pay for car repairs, and she'd bank whatever else she earned. No reason she couldn't save up money without Mark or her dad urging her to do so. Enough about Mark. She was at the mall with another friend.

Antonio adjusted his blue San Diego Chargers cap. It reminded her of when Mark and Chris played football in high school. She had cheered for the Beaumont Junior High team, but she still got to watch the high school guys warm up. Sort of what precipitated the Valentine's Day debacle.

She gazed at Antonio. It didn't matter anymore. At the moment, it looked as though she might not be alone when February 14 rolled around. Maybe the two of them could hang out and do something friendly.

"Wanna go to the movies now?" Antonio asked.

Beth sighed. "Yeah, but I really should start these applications."

Antonio smirked. "Live a little. Have fun."

Guilt got the best of Beth. Antonio had given her rides to and from school, made sure his mechanic friend didn't overcharge her for repairs, and had come to the mall with her. "OK, but just this once." Beth walked with Antonio toward the movie theater, passing by the food court along the way. The smell of pepperoni pizza permeated throughout—the same scent as the Beaumont Mall. Maybe food courts everywhere smelled the same.

After they'd paid for their tickets, settled into their seats, and the previews started, Beth caught a glimpse of Antonio grinning at her. While Mark was serious, Antonio proved to be the opposite. No worries, no cares. Being around him was fun, life on the go. And being just friends—friends who didn't share a past—removed any pressure. Still a nagging sense of something missing plagued her.

෬෧

The winds outside had been stronger than usual. Mark straightened his gale-swept hair then took the change the concession worker handed him and slipped it into his pocket. Why did everything cost twice as much at the theater? He took a sip of his soft drink then shook the container. Eighty percent ice. Nice.

Tim led the way down the movie aisle. He pointed to a couple in the distance. "Hey, there's Beth with that guy."

Mark put up his hand. "Don't wave."

"Why not?"

He released a sigh. "Because she's on a date."

"So?"

"So leave her alone." While Mark handled the accounting at Fishy Business, he could calculate more than the books. He'd called it. Maybe he was off by a week or two, but he could tell the guy was into Beth by how he'd first looked at her. A mental kick assailed him. He should have spoken up earlier, told her how he felt.

Tim leaned toward him. "When are you going to tell her?"

"She doesn't come around the store much anymore, and things have worked out OK since she left. Why dredge up unpleasant memories? Besides, she appears to be dating, having fun. Why ruin her life?"

"Are you afraid talking to her about what happened might...?"

He shrugged. "Trigger an episode? Uh, yeah."

"I think you'd feel better if you tell her."

There was no sense in even entertaining the thought. Maybe talking about it would help *him*. But what about her? Better to leave Beth alone and not confuse or upset her. He'd ruined two lives already, why mess up a third? If Mark really cared for her, he'd let her be.

What's-his-name did the stretch and yawn routine to put his arm behind Beth. *Puh-lease.* Mark's shoulders tensed. Why did it bother him so much? Was it a protective instinct? Not really. The guy wasn't exactly being a jerk. The most he'd seen him do was touch her shoulder. No, something else. Mark cracked his knuckles. The green-eyed monster, perhaps?

But what if Beth's boyfriend was the White Knight? Hadn't the notes stopped coming right before she started seeing the guy?

Tim moved to the wheelchair access row in the middle of the theater.

Mark wished there was a little more distance between him and Beth. He could be happy for her, but that didn't mean he needed to watch her get cozy with someone else.

The opening credits rolled. A few minutes passed. An explosion then a car chase scene. So far, so good.

Mark glanced over at Beth. She hadn't clung to her date during the scary part. A good sign. He leaned toward Tim. "You think he could be the one?"

"The one what?" Tim asked. "You think he's gonna pop the question to her or something?"

"I mean the one who wrote her those notes."

Tim took a sip of his soda. "He could be. But anyone could for that matter. Like Randy, for instance. He's pretty chummy with Beth."

"If we're suspecting everyone who's friendly to

Beth, I'd have to add both of our names to the suspect list. Besides, how could Randy get the notes to her at work?"

"That's a good point. It does make Beth's boy toy seem suspicious."

"Boy toy?" Mark stared and hoped Tim felt the full weight of the glare.

Mark glanced over at Beth. She'd exited his world by her own choice. Should he follow her to ensure her safety, or did he leave her be?

Mark shifted his gaze to the movie screen. The hero slammed his brakes, yet the car skidded into a concrete barrier. Bleeding from his forehead, he climbed out of the mangled vehicle and helped the leading lady escape from the passenger side. Together, they limped away as the villain approached. The villain insisted he belonged with the leading lady. Just like the notes from the Knight.

Run! Don't let him catch you. A shiver ran down his spine.

The theater grew pitch black. Small lights lit the floor along the aisle. Tim stood, holding his cell phone. "All the high wind tonight must have knocked out the power."

A while later, he and Tim exited the building.

"Of all the nights the Santa Ana winds could have swept through the valley." Mark crossed his arms. "I really wanted to see the end of that."

"At least they gave us rain checks. We can come back tomorrow night." Tim walked away then stopped. "Wait." He held up his hand, blocking Mark's path.

Mark tried to peek around his friend. "What is it?"

Tim contorted his face. "Some couple. I think they

might kiss."

"So?" He pushed Tim aside. Oh. He meant *that* couple. Beth and the other teacher, standing outside, close to each other.

Mark clenched his fists. "Well, Tim, in case you hadn't noticed, that's what couples do." He moved forward, far enough away from Beth that she shouldn't see him. Tim stayed close behind.

Maybe this was God's way of saving Beth from heartache. If she'd gotten closer to Mark, he'd only let her down with all his deception.

His cell vibrated, and he glanced down. No incoming call. Just a text message from earlier. His phone must have just picked up reception outside the theater.

HI, MARK. CAN WE MEET FOR BREAKFAST BEFORE CLASS ON MONDAY? I'D LIKE TO DISCUSS A FEW THINGS. WHY DON'T YOU PICK A TIME AND PLACE AND GET BACK WITH ME? CAROL.

A text from one of the women he and his friends had dined with previously. He'd seen her on campus a few times. She taught a special education class at Riversdale Community College. Interesting. She must have gotten his number from Bill or Tim. Where was this headed—a friendly gesture and nothing more? Perhaps.

He bit back a grin and puffed out his chest. Perhaps not.

21

The Knight stared at his yellow memo pad. A crease marred the top paper. He ripped it off and tossed it atop the pile of wadded papers he'd thrown earlier in the evening. He stared at the bottle of pills on the desk. Magical modern marvels that helped him cope long enough to get through his nine-to-five. The creases in the papers continued to irritate him. Maybe he should take his meds. No, home was his domain. No need to kowtow to society's notions of normal while inside his own castle. It was bad enough he'd had to force himself to take pills for work and the few times he attended a support group—something that turned out to be a complete waste of time.

He tossed the notepad in the trash. Beth no longer hung out with Mark. No sense in writing her more notes. Sure the Knight still cared about her, but his reason for writing the notes had ceased to exist. Yet he'd continue to watch over her, to protect her from any threats.

The Knight stared at the photo of his dear friend. Poor Juanita. She should have learned her lesson like Beth.

But what if Beth went back to Mark? That would be a grave mistake.

Speaking of which, perhaps it was time to visit Juanita over in Plot Fifty. If he left now, he could be at Riversdale Cemetery in ten minutes.

But he'd never have to take things that far with someone as smart as Beth.

She'd stay far away from Mark Graham if she knew what was good for her. Otherwise, the Knight would be forced to take drastic measures. Good thing she had someone like him to look out for her.

Not everyone was so fortunate.

22

A week had passed since Beth's last outing with Antonio. He arrived at the food court of the Riversdale Mall to enjoy dinner with her during her evening work break. Beth wanted to try the Chinese buffet but hadn't been able to talk Antonio into it yet. Instead, they dined on cheeseburgers and fries.

Beth wiped her mouth with the corner of her napkin. If only life could slow down long enough for her to catch up. "My life's so crazy right now with teaching and the drama club. And once spring nears and it's time for the annual play, it'll only get worse. Though I guess your life is hectic too during football season."

Antonio grinned, then took a sip of his soda. "So you think maybe we could see another movie this weekend?"

"I'll have to see what my schedule for next week is like. But yeah, that'd be fun."

Antonio's eyes widened. He became animated, using hand gestures. "There's this new sci-fi movie coming out. *Your Mom is from Mars.* A lot of big name stars are in it. I'm sure you've seen the previews."

Not exactly what she had in mind. But at least he was company.

For the remainder of their meal, Beth asked Antonio about his football team, and he was more than eager to provide her with details.

While Antonio chatted, a couple walked by, holding a painting of a battle scene. They must have visited the Paintings and Posters store on the other side of the mall. Beth didn't recognize the battle, but Mark would know. Yep, Professor Graham had the lowdown on all things historical. Sometimes she missed hearing him spout off facts.

Antonio slurped his soft drink. "So I hope you'll come to the game tomorrow."

Beth glanced at the clock hanging on the opposite wall. "I'm sorry. I really have to go, but I appreciate you stopping by." She stood and emptied her trash at a nearby receptacle, stacking her tray on top of others.

Antonio did the same then walked with Beth back to California Chic.

As she headed toward the register, Antonio waved good-bye then left.

For a few minutes, the store experienced a lull in customers. Beth helped her bubbly blonde coworker fold sweaters and set them on a table. Beth folded a blue cardigan then peered out into the mall.

Directly across from her store, Tim and a brunette sat close on a bench, while a blonde lounged on his other side. Beth could hear Mark but couldn't see him. Her shoulders tensed. What was he doing there?

In a voice loud enough she could make out parts of his conversation, he told a funny story about the history of the mall's carousel. Judging from the sound of the blonde woman's laugh, she appreciated his sense of humor. Who wouldn't? Beth stole a second look. The woman didn't resemble a supermodel, but she wasn't hideous either.

Beth's coworker turned toward her. "I have to get some more inventory from the back. It'll only take a second."

If he came into the store, they'd have to talk. Her stomach tightened. "I need to stretch my legs. I'll go get it. How many boxes?"

Her coworker tilted her head. "Two. They're sitting by the door. Are you sure?"

Beth nodded as she strode away. She reached the storage area and flung open the door. Inside, she leaned against the wall and breathed a sigh of relief. That was close.

So Mark was happy and found someone else— someone closer to his age. Great. But she didn't need to see them together. Besides, given their past history and the way he'd treated her, it shouldn't bother her anyway.

23

Talk about a long day. So much for Beth's bright idea to get middle school kids to read Shakespeare. Quite an exercise in futility.

She walked into her apartment and set her bag and purse on her kitchen counter then sniffed her sleeve. Did her entire place smell like a middle school or only her? The scent of cheap cologne mingled with teen sweat assaulted her senses.

A light flashed on her answering machine. Maybe her parents called. Or perhaps Mark. She released a breath she hadn't realized she'd been holding. As if Mark had even thought about her during the past few weeks. She tapped the play button. A long beep sounded, and a message followed.

"It's Antonio. Give me a call when you get a chance. Thanks."

In three weeks' time, she'd become exhausted. Tired of doing stuff with him while trying to work two jobs. At first it was natural to hang out with him, but then she questioned why he'd become so friendly. Like leaning way too close to her outside the movie theater. Friends didn't stand *that* close.

She dialed his number. "Antonio?"

"Hey, I got your message. I'm sorry we couldn't go out last week or this week, but maybe—"

"Wait, before you say anything else, I need to say something." She lowered her voice. "You're a good friend, Antonio, and we've had fun together. But, I'm afraid that maybe I've given you the impression that I'm interested in a relationship, which just isn't the case."

Antonio was silent. She had no way of gauging his reaction.

She cleared her throat. "Are you OK?"

"Are you sure you don't want to hang out anymore?"

"We can still be friends, but I don't want to lead you on."

"I—I don't know what to say. I didn't realize you felt this way. I was hoping we could hang out as friends, but it sounds like you've already made up your mind. Guess I'll see you around." He hung up.

Beth realized she didn't feel sad or upset. Instead, relief flooded over her.

The notes from the Knight had stopped, and she'd be safe, with or without Mark or Antonio.

24

Beth shook her head. "*It's* is not possessive." She wielded her red pen then entered the student's information in her grade book. One of Antonio's darlings. The boy wouldn't get to play in the next game—not with a D plus on his English assignment.

She'd only run into Antonio twice that week, not too awkward though. Beth would inform Antonio of his student's ineligibility first thing the next morning. She set down her red pen and took a much-needed break from grading papers.

The pink hue from the setting sun lit up the evening sky outside her living room window. An urge to close her blinds overcame her. Perhaps staying up late the night before reading a novel about a serial killer wasn't the best idea. She scanned the area in front of her apartment before shutting her blinds. What if the Knight *was* out there, watching her every move? She shook her head, willing away the thoughts of what if.

Talking to someone else would help her stay grounded in reality. Even with the time difference, her parents should still be up. She grabbed her phone off the coffee table. A few weeks had passed since she'd last spoken to them. "Hey, Dad. It's good to hear your voice."

"Hey, kiddo. How have you been?"

She considered mentioning the notes from the

Knight. But they'd stopped coming. No reason to make Dad worry.

Forcing herself to relax, Beth kicked off her shoes and swung her feet up on her couch. "Fine."

"That's good to hear, and how's Mark? Did you two catch the Ohio State game on Saturday?"

Her neck muscles tightened. "No, we didn't. I've been so busy I haven't really spoken to Mark lately." A truthful statement, more or less. She'd been busy...avoiding him.

"You know, it's almost Thanksgiving. Mom's been shelving her scrapbooks and getting out her recipe books."

Beth scratched her head. Coming home would be fun. Fun but expensive. "Yeah, Dad, about that. I don't think I'll be able to come home for Thanksgiving this year, but maybe Christmas or during spring break."

"Your mom and I love you, and although we'd love to see you, we understand." His voice lowered a decibel. "Like you said, maybe we can see each other at Christmas."

"Thanks, Dad." Beth spent twenty more minutes on the phone with him, reminiscing and catching up. Then she headed for bed. Why did she miss her parents so much? *Dear God, please provide a way for me to see them.*

25

Beth shut off her computer, stuffed her grade book in her bag, and made sure to lock her desk before leaving her classroom. She opened the door and stepped into the nearly deserted hallway.

"Beth?"

Antonio approached her.

"I need to tell you something. It's sort of—"

"Sort of what?" She adjusted her bag on her shoulder.

"I don't know how to tell you this, but…" Antonio checked the hallway, but no one else was there. "Long story, but I saw one of my players in the parking lot of this physical therapy center near my gym. I chatted with him and ended up following him inside. And, it's really weird, but—"

"But what?"

"I saw your friend Mark inside of this place, and he was walking."

Ten years earlier, when Beth had passed Mark in front of the Hometown Café, even then, he was in a wheelchair. Quite a shock considering she hadn't known he'd been injured. How could he suddenly walk? It didn't make sense. Unless…Could Mark be leading a double life? "Walking? Are you sure? He's been in a wheelchair for several years. It had to be someone else. Maybe someone who just looks like him?"

Antonio threw his arms in the air. "Maybe. But it looked an awful lot like him." He marched away.

Maybe Antonio thought he saw Mark, but clearly he was mistaken. It wasn't like Mark to keep a secret from her. Perhaps Antonio was jealous and wanted to make Mark look bad somehow. Antonio once made the comment that she talked about Mark a lot.

Or maybe Mr. Coach was angry one of his players was ineligible. Tough. Football wasn't everything. Try getting a job without knowing how to read or write.

If he made up a story about someone with a physical disability, that was pretty low. Maybe it was a blessing that things hadn't gotten serious between her and Antonio.

Come to think of it, she started receiving strange notes around the same time she met him. Maybe he was the one leaving them on her desk and in her bag. The notes stopped coming right before they'd started hanging out. He certainly had ample opportunity. But what was his motive—to make her scared and run into his arms? Who knew what made men behave like that. Perhaps she should confront him about the notes sometime.

Beth left the school and passed Fishy Business on her way home. Maybe it was time to pay Mark and the guys a visit. She pulled into the parking lot and headed toward the entry. Randy waved as he left his truck and walked toward the building.

Tim came out the front door and picked up a phone book left on the front mat then went back inside. Maybe he hadn't seen her. There was still time to walk away before she might run into Mark and the blonde. The sight would be hard to stomach. Confused and torn, she hurried back to her car and continued home.

26

So Beth still had an interest in Mark Graham. To think, she was the smart one. The Knight shook his head. He had her best interests in mind, really.

He opened his desk drawer. Out of yellow notes! The Knight slammed the drawer shut then headed to the dining room.

A notebook lay on his table. After tearing a page from the book, he fought the urge to fling it across the room. He couldn't make a mess. The Knight stared at the page. The jagged edges irked him. A bottle of pills sat in the distance. The medication had lasted through the work day but by now had worn off.

He grabbed the notebook and took his time removing a page. The paper tore in one spot. A string of curses spewed from his lips, and he folded the first two sheets of paper. He couldn't crumple them. The Knight stared at his clenched fists then took a deep breath. His hands trembled as he separated a perforated page from the notebook.

He took a moment to relight the candles surrounding his shrine to Beth. Gaining inspiration, he admired her photo. A chill ran over him. What if Beth refused his help?

He stared in the direction of his gun safe. Be a shame to waste such a beautiful life. Besides, Plot Fifty was taken.

To be fair, the Knight would warn Beth about

possible repercussions of refusing his assistance. If she was smarter than Juanita, she'd take the hint. Sweat trickled down his face. He steadied his hand enough to compose the letter. Anticipation flooding over him, he could hardly wait to leave Beth her next surprise.

27

Another day closer to Thanksgiving. And Beth hadn't run into Antonio all day. Probably good considering the big football game scheduled that evening, and one of his little stars wouldn't be playing. Sometime soon, she needed to confront him about the notes. Maybe after school, when fewer people would be around. Being a new teacher, she didn't want to make a scene. It was only Antonio. She had no reason to fear him. Still, a sense of unease overcame her as she walked alone to her car and drove away from the school.

Beth entered her apartment, closed the door behind her, and set her bag on the coffee table. Her grade book slid out. No big deal. She had all night to put it back in place.

As she stumbled into her kitchen, the phone rang. "Hello?"

"Hey, honey, it's Dad. Mom and I talked it over. We've been saving up frequent flyer miles, and we've decided to fly out to California to see you for Thanksgiving. Mom purchased our tickets today."

Beth squealed. "Seriously? Where are you flying into?"

"Orange County Airport."

Orange County. Also known as John Wayne Airport. *Ugh.* Mark's trivial facts invaded her brain. Before she could chide herself for thinking about him, her father interrupted her thoughts.

"Our flight arrives at 9:00 PM the day before Thanksgiving."

"Great, I'll be there. I can't wait to see both of you. I'm so excited." Nine PM. or 2100 hours. She rubbed her forehead. Corporal Mark Graham had permeated her train of thought. She scribbled the time on a notepad.

"Are you sure you don't mind picking us up? We could rent a car."

"Huh?" *Stop thinking about him.* Beth grabbed a pen from a cup on her kitchen counter and circled the flight date on her calendar. "Not at all."

"Great. We can't wait to see you, sweetie."

Beth dropped the pen back in the cup. "I can't wait to see you guys either. I would have been bummed if I had to spend Thanksgiving alone. Guess I would have hung out with my friends or done something else, but it wouldn't have been the same."

"I'm glad we're coming. I couldn't stand to think of you being lonely. That reminds me, does Mark have somewhere to go?"

Beth stepped into her living room. "Mark? Oh, I don't know." She cleared her throat. "I've been so busy I haven't had time to talk to him."

Silence. Beth kicked off her shoes and plopped down on the couch, tucking her legs underneath her. "What's the matter, Dad?"

"He doesn't have any family left, and I worry about him."

Maybe he didn't have anyone. Or did he? The blonde at the mall flicked through her mind. Beth ran her fuchsia fingernails along the edge of the coffee table—the one Mark's friends had helped her move.

She released a sigh. "Tell you what, Dad. I'll find out what his plans are for Thanksgiving, OK?"

"He could certainly join us for dinner. We don't mind."

So true. They didn't mind. Mark had been like a permanent fixture at their house while growing up. Both good and bad.

"Oh. Mom finished making dinner. I better go. I'll talk to you later, honey. We look forward to seeing you."

Beth hung up the phone. Was she really going to spend Thanksgiving with her family?

She picked up her lesson planner. As Beth shoved the planner in her bag, a folded sheet of notebook paper fell out and fluttered through the air, landing under her coffee table. She'd recorded all her grades. Maybe it was a student assignment that had become lodged in there—one she hadn't returned. Bending to pick it up, her back ached. She decided to leave it where it was. The paper could wait until later. Besides, she wasn't dying to meet the dust bunnies living under her table.

She had more important things to do. Like planning Thanksgiving dinner.

As she headed toward her bedroom, the yearbook on the coffee table caught her attention. She'd better take it over to Marisa before she forgot.

❧

Beth knocked and waited. No sign of her friend right away, so she opened the yearbook and stared at the signatures.

Marisa opened the door. "Hey, come on in. Sorry

to keep you waiting."

Why dredge up unpleasant memories of her teenage crush by looking at photos? Beth closed the yearbook and trailed her friend to the kitchen.

Marisa finished loading two pans into her dishwasher then closed the door, revealing a cat magnet on the front indicating the dishes were dirty. The dishwasher rumbled as she turned it on before she glanced at Beth's yearbook. "Beaumont High? Is that yours?"

She nodded. Good old Beaumont. Maybe Mark was homesick, too. She could at least check on him, for her dad's sake. All she needed was a way to find out how he was doing without having to run into him and his blonde friend. She handed Marisa the book. "Here. You needed yearbooks."

"Thanks."

A plan on how to check up on Mark brewed in her mind. "Don't thank me yet. I need a favor."

Marisa moved toward the living room. "What is it?"

She needed to convince Marisa to go along with the plan. Beth grabbed a pad and pen from the kitchen. After scribbling a number on the paper, she handed it to her friend. "Can you call this number and ask for Tim Wilson? If he picks up, hand me the phone. If someone else answers, say you'll call back later then hang up."

Marisa glanced at the paper then back at Beth and chuckled. "Do I want to know why? I'm not involved in something illegal, am I?"

Beth shook her head. "Nothing like that. Look, it's a long story."

Marisa's eyes widened. She dialed the number and

strolled into the living room, away from the chugging of the dishwasher.

Beth followed.

"Hello," Marisa said. "May I please speak to Tim Wilson? Hi—"

Good, Mark hadn't answered. Just what she'd wanted. Beth took the phone from her friend. "Hey, Tim. It's Beth. I wanted to call and check up on the corporal, no big deal. Anyway, I thought I'd talk to you."

"Why don't you come over and—"

"That's OK. I'm really busy, and besides, he probably wouldn't tell me how he really is, right?" Beth paced the living room.

"And I will?"

She could hear him munching in the background. Probably eating chips. "Yeah. So how is he? Do you know if he has any plans for Thanksgiving?"

Tim lowered his voice. "He seems to be OK. He's been working a lot lately. And as for Thanksgiving, our family invites him over every year, but he usually stays at home."

"Really?"

"Yep, he always spends the holidays alone."

"OK, I have to go, but thanks."

"You should stop by sometime. We miss you."

"We" meaning Tim, or "we" meaning Mark and the others? "I'll do that, but for now, I'd appreciate it if you wouldn't mention I called. Bye." Beth hung up the phone.

There. Mark had opportunities, even if he didn't take advantage of them. Besides, if he didn't join his best friends for the holidays, why would he consider coming to her apartment and eating with her family?

She hadn't been at Fishy Business in weeks, and it wasn't like he'd called to ask her how she was doing. For all he knew, she could have received more notes from the Knight. Sure, she hadn't called him either. But that was different.

Marisa stared at her. "That phone call—care to elaborate?"

Beth slumped onto Marisa's couch. "My dad asked me to check on Mark. I wanted to find out if he has any plans for Thanksgiving."

Marisa sat down beside her. "Well, does he?"

It wasn't her fault Mark chose not to spend Thanksgiving with Bill and Tim's family each year. Beth folded her hands and studied Marisa's coffee table, admiring the small white doily in the center. "His friends invite him over, but he usually refuses. Maybe he prefers to spend Thanksgiving alone."

Marisa wrinkled her forehead. "Would you?"

She shook her head. "Not really." Mark's parents were gone. Chris was gone. The blonde—well, maybe the woman had left the picture, too. Sort of like Beth had. Bottom line, no one was around. People like Antonio—those who had never lost anyone close to them—couldn't understand Mark's loneliness. But Beth did.

She fidgeted with the dog tags around her neck. Like the lead in a certain old Broadway musical, there were times she wanted to wash this guy out of her life, but no matter what, their paths were destined to continually cross.

Marisa glanced at her.

"You think I should invite him to my apartment for Thanksgiving?" He'd probably give her some excuse, a reason as to why he had to stay and work at the store, some sort of obligation.

She chewed an already abused nail. An obligation. Mark was a Marine, and a man of honor would be bound by obligation. Yes, of course. Would her plan work? "He'd just say no unless..."

Marisa leaned closer. "Unless what?"

Beth stood up. "I can't talk. I have to make a phone call. I'll see you later." She jetted out the door toward her own apartment.

Once inside, she grabbed her car keys and bent down to pick up the paper hiding under the coffee table. In the process, she knocked over a glass of water near the table's edge. The glass rolled off the table. Water splashed everywhere, including on the note. At least she'd already recorded the grade, because the paper was now ruined. Good thing she was passing out grade printouts tomorrow. Either way, the student would see his grade. He didn't need a soggy paper. She crumpled and tossed the notebook paper in the trash. Somehow the glass hadn't broken. She carried it to the kitchen.

For the second time, she left her apartment and got in her car, headed toward Riversdale with a plan in mind. Who knew? By the time Thanksgiving rolled around, she might even have forgotten about what happened during her eighth grade year. Anything was possible.

ॐ∽

As she exited her vehicle outside Fishy Business, Beth ignored the gentle roar of traffic and relaxed her shoulders for the first time that Monday evening. While the news about the pay raise invigorated her, it'd been a long day. At least Thanksgiving was around the corner.

She shifted her gaze to the pink envelope in her hand. Her fingers grasped the perfect obligation, one she hoped Mark couldn't ignore.

With great care, she smoothed her blouse and ran her fingers through her hair. Not having been to Fishy Business in weeks, she could have at least refreshed her makeup before showing up.

Gaining a slight swing in her step, she walked to the rear entrance, pink envelope and a small plastic container in hand, and anticipated the look of surprise on Mark's face. She twisted the knob, but it was locked, so she knocked on the door. "Anyone there?"

Tim answered wearing a white apron. "Beth?" He smiled. "Good to see you. It's been awhile. Glad you decided to stop by." Placing a hand on her shoulder, he leaned in and hugged her.

Beth inhaled the familiar scent of nacho cheese. Mark wasn't the only one she had avoided. By staying away, she'd missed seeing all of her friends.

Tim scratched his head. "Mark's not here. He and Bill went to the movies. Bill talked him into seeing some sci-fi flick." He strode over to the cash register and locked the drawer.

She set down the container and envelope and leaned her hands on the counter. "He's..." She willed herself not to frown. "They're both gone?"

The front store sign indicated the store was closed.

Tim looked at the green fish clock on the far wall. "Yeah, but they should be back around eleven."

A memo pad sat on Mark's desk. It reminded her of the Knight. She stepped closer to examine it. Rectangular. About the same shade of yellow. Same lines on the paper.

"Something the matter, Beth?"

She turned.

Tim held a knife in his hand.

She flinched then clamped one hand to her chest.

He lowered the knife to his side. "Sorry if I scared you. I was going to gut some fish. You OK? You seem jumpy."

She could explain to him that the Knight had written his messages to her on yellow notes, which explained her concern. But that was silly. As if anyone at Fishy Business was out to get her.

Another thought brewed in her mind as she rejoined Tim by the counter. So no one else was around. Perhaps this was her golden opportunity. Beth glanced at her watch. Ten forty-five. "Mark won't be back until later? Actually, that's even better."

Tim unwrapped two fish from butcher paper on the counter and held up his knife. "What do you mean?"

"I've wanted to ask you something." She glanced around the store in case Mark or Bill had slipped in. Gathering strength, she lowered her voice. "But I never wanted to ask with Mark around, or Bill either." She touched Tim on the forearm to get his attention then stared at him. "I want to know the truth about what happened to Chris. You were there, right?"

Tim nodded. "I was, but do you really want to know?"

"Yes." She played with her nails. "How did he die? No one told me. My folks are silent on the subject."

Tim rested the knife next to the fish, rubbed his hands on his apron, and released a sigh.

Why was it so hard to get the truth out of everyone? The more they kept quiet, the harder it was for her to move beyond her brother's death. Sure, her parents knew more than she did, but they wouldn't discuss it with her. And she couldn't put them through that.

Tim grabbed the fish and resumed gutting.

Beth tapped her nails on the weathered butcher block counter, careful to avoid splinters. "Bill's not around. Mark's not around, so you're not going to upset them. I feel as if I deserve to know what happened to my brother. If something happened to Bill, you'd want to know more."

"Sometimes we think we want to know the truth, but…" Tim laid the knife on the counter. "Sometimes the truth hurts."

Arms folded, she bit her lip. "Sometimes not knowing hurts just as much."

Tim leaned toward her. "The mission was supposed to be a simple recon, but we were ambushed. We came under heavy fire later in the evening. Chris was near the front of the formation and got hit. Mark grabbed him and carried him to safety, but it was too late."

Tim grabbed a second fish and began gutting. "You've heard of captains going down with their sinking ships?"

"Yeah, of course. Like on the *Titanic*."

"As corporal, Mark did what he could to make sure all of us came back safely. So you can see why it was hard for him when Chris died. Mark did what he could, but not enough in his mind, which explains his condition."

She began to step closer, but after eyeing the

putrid remains of the fish, decided to keep her distance. There was a reason she taught English and drama and not biology. "What do you mean?"

Tim set down the knife and gripped the counter with both hands. His cheeks flushed.

Mark had wheeled in and now stared at them, a smile on his face. "What are you doing?"

Bill walked over to the desk, sat down, and removed a comic book from a plastic bag.

Tim stepped forward, but she put out her hand to stop him. "I came by, and you weren't here. It gave Tim and me the opportunity to discuss Chris's death."

Disappointment and hurt shone from Mark's eyes.

What did it hurt for Tim to tell her what happened? And what was Mark hiding from her? His condition? Antonio claimed to have seen Mark walking. Was there some truth to that? But why wouldn't he want to tell her? "It's OK, Mark. I asked him. I wanted to know. Tim didn't—"

He pointed at her. "No, you think you do, but you don't. I was there when Chris died and would like to forget it, but I never can, not completely." Eyes wide open, he looked at Beth. "You're young. You're impulsive. You're going to make poor decisions. I get that." He shot daggers at Tim. "But you, Private..."

Beth glared at Mark, her hands firmly planted on her hips. "What is that supposed to mean? I'm going to make poor decisions? I'm not a kid anymore."

"A few weeks ago you were worried about money, yet you run off to the mall with your boyfriend."

She rolled her eyes at him. "The mall? My boyfriend? You don't even—Ugh!" She gritted her teeth. "Never mind. It's not like you'd understand." She pointed to Tim. "And don't blame him. At least he doesn't withhold information."

Mark gripped the armrests of his wheelchair. "This is between Tim and me. Stay out of it."

Beth raised her voice. Her lip quivered. "Oh, I will. I'll be sure to stay far away."

Mark glared at Tim.

Beth gathered the pink envelope and plastic container and scurried toward the back of the store. Her reason for coming was irrelevant now. She placed the envelope and container on the desk. "This is for Mark." She wiped her eye with her sleeve. "Not that he'll care anyway, but in case he asks."

Bill nodded and went back to reading his comic book.

With great force, she slammed the door shut on her way out. Once inside her car, she slumped into the driver's seat and doubled over, shaking as she sobbed. She held her head in her hands.

What just happened? In one moment, their friendship had ended.

❧◆❧

Mark ended his verbal barrage with Tim and wheeled to the back of the store. He spied a pink envelope on top of a plastic container, snatched it from the desk, and shoved it in Bill's face. "What's this?"

Bill shrugged. "Beth left it. I have no idea what's inside, other than she said it was for you."

Mark tore open the envelope and removed the contents. "It's an invitation to Thanksgiving dinner at her apartment with her family." He showed it to his friend. "Why would she invite me?"

Bill threw up his hands. "Why don't you ask her?"

Mark opened the plastic container. Buckeyes. Chocolate treats with a peanut butter center. Just like the ones they'd buy at the front counter of the Hometown Café when they were kids. He sampled one. Tasted as good as the ones from back home, too.

He'd berated her, and here she'd done something nice for him. Kicking himself, he ran his fingers through his hair. Ouch. He couldn't blame her if she dishonorably discharged him from her life and never spoke to him again.

Mark slipped outside and craned his neck. The Big Dipper lit the night sky. He moved over to the security light and looked at the envelope. His name was written in cursive red ink. Such perfectly formed letters. A strange sense overcame him, a feeling this had happened before, like déjà vu. He lifted the envelope to his nose—a floral fragrance—Beth's perfume.

Once a Marine, always a Marine. For someone who knew better, his actions had been less than honorable.

After a glance at his watch, he scrambled home. The only thing worse than disappointing one woman was letting down two.

He'd promised Carol he'd meet her for breakfast again, and he needed to get to sleep so he could get up on time. Before getting in bed, he studied the pink envelope on his nightstand. Why did that writing appear familiar? Perhaps he'd seen Beth's writing at the store or in a letter to Chris. Sitting up and mulling over it wouldn't help. He got in bed and turned off the light.

When 6:00 AM rolled around, he met Carol at the Sunshine Diner over on Fifth Street.

This morning marked his third breakfast with her.

He took a sip of his coffee. Plain and boring.

A thin redheaded waitress walked by. He flagged her down. "Excuse me, ma'am, you wouldn't happen to have any flavored coffee, hazelnut, perhaps?"

"No, I'm sorry, we don't." The redhead smiled and walked away.

Carol said something.

He smiled, nodded, and hoped that was the appropriate response to whatever she'd said. Not that he didn't care or want to listen, but more important thoughts took precedence.

While he sat there doing nothing, the Knight could still be harassing Beth. He'd ticked her off pretty good the night before. If his actions caused her to get closer to that guy... *Breathe.* He wanted to check on her, but pride—or was it the fear of admitting he cared—stopped him.

Carol leaned across the table toward him. "So you'll help me write the grant for more funding?"

Oh, boy. Was that what he'd nodded and agreed to? "Sure, I'd be glad to help." So word about his grant-writing experience had made its way across campus. He hadn't seen that coming. Perhaps that was the only reason Carol had befriended him.

The waitress walked over and set the bill on the table.

Carol snatched the paper. "Thanks. This one's on me. See you at school." She removed several bills from her wallet, set them on the table, then stood up and left.

Mark stared at his cup. It wasn't only the coffee; life, in general, had lost its flavor.

Funny it'd taken him this long to realize he liked hazelnut. Good thing he knew where to find it.

28

Mark didn't want to remember the night Chris died, and neither should Beth. He could only imagine what Tim told her about his episodes—and about how her brother died. Secrets that should have gone to the grave.

Sure Beth befriended him when he was in the chair, but what about now? What happened if she'd found out his problem was emotional, not physical? Maybe she could accept useless legs, but what about a useless mind? And what else had Tim told her? Not everything, not all the gory details, right?

Mark inhaled one last whiff of the floral perfume, dropped the envelope in his lap, and covered his face with his hands. Hurting Beth Martindale—the one thing he'd tried to avoid, and he'd been unsuccessful. *Lord, help me. I don't want to lose her.*

Mark drove to the Playa Del Sol apartments Tuesday afternoon and knocked on Beth's door. No one answered. He couldn't blame her for shutting him out after the way he had treated her. He began to leave. As he rolled away, he ran into a young, short-haired brunette who was walking near Beth's apartment. "Excuse me. Do you know where Beth is?"

The woman stared at him.

Mark put out his hand. "I'm Mark Graham. I'm friends with—"

She nodded and shook his hand. "I know who you

are. I'm Marisa."

So this was Beth's friend, the one she wanted to set him up with. No offense to her friend, but he found Beth more attractive. Then again, he could be biased. "Oh, nice to meet you."

"I live next door. You can come in for a minute if you'd like." Marisa opened her door.

He followed her inside to her living room and wheeled next to her couch. If Beth had told Marisa what had happened, she'd probably think he was a jerk, too. Great. He glanced at the black cat clock on the wall. Its eyes moved, and the tail wagged. On an end table sat a jar of potpourri. The overpowering apple cinnamon scent attacked his sinuses.

"If you're looking for Beth," Marisa said. "She's not here. She's at the mall."

Why had he accused her of spending money there? He shouldn't care what she did with her cash. "Oh, with Pedro, or whatever his name is?"

Marisa shook her head. "Antonio? No. Didn't she tell you? They're not dating. In fact, they're not even hanging out anymore. Ever since Beth got a second job at the mall, all she does is save her money and—"

"She's working at the mall?" So she was single and worked a second job.

Marisa nodded. "Yeah, a lot of teachers have second jobs. Beth wants to save up extra money." Marisa studied the piece of paper in Mark's hand. "What's that?"

He held it up. "It's an invitation."

Marisa smiled. "So she talked you into joining her for Thanksgiving dinner?"

"What do you mean?"

Marisa slouched in her seat. "Her dad asked about

you. He wanted to know if you had plans for Thanksgiving. Beth was afraid if she asked you, you'd just say no."

"So, her family wanted me to come. That's…that's nice." So it was her dad's idea. That made more sense.

"Well, maybe not the *only* reason."

What other reason was there besides pity? He leaned closer. "Meaning?"

Marisa shook her head. "I tried to tell her, but she didn't believe me."

He folded his hands. "Tell her what?"

"C'mon, you're a professor. You can figure this out."

He stared at the ground. "Does this have something to do with the incident on the boat?" He'd replayed the event in his mind recently, trying to determine what had gone wrong.

"When she hooked her finger? Yeah. When she came to my apartment that day, she seemed very confused. I suggested she thought of you as more than a friend. Beth sort of freaked out."

So being accused of liking him was that mortifying to Beth, so much so that it freaked her out. Not good. His shoulders tensed.

Mark gazed at her bookcase. "You actually own books by Solzhenitsyn?" Though his life could never compare with the author, in many ways, Mark's secrets confined him. He desired to be free from his prison.

"Yes, have you read them?"

"As a matter of fact, I have. I teach history over at Riversdale Community College."

"Beth mentioned you worked there, but I didn't know you taught history." Marisa's eyes twinkled. "I teach social studies, too, but to high school students."

"Now see, I knew you were a teacher, but I didn't know what you taught." Mark glanced at his watch. "It was nice meeting you." He glanced at her table. Two yearbooks lie on top. One of them, a copy of *Buckeyes*. He pointed. "The yearbook from the school Beth and I attended. How'd you get that?"

"Oh, she let me borrow it. I was trying to get ideas for our school's yearbook."

"Mind if I ...?" He picked it up.

"Not at all. In fact, I'm finished with it. I don't think Beth would mind if you want to borrow it."

"Thanks." He waved good-bye then left. The yearbook was in his hands. It might be fun to remember things the way they used to be. Also, it presented the perfect opportunity to discover Beth's crush. Not that it mattered much now.

He mustn't tease her about anything. In fact, he should do something nice. Set things right. A few of the guys who'd been on the Beaumont Junior High football team when he was a senior owed him favors. Maybe he could arrange for her to meet the man of her dreams, assuming she was even still interested in the guy after all these years. The least he could do.

29

The Knight scribbled in his notebook.

4:00 PM—Mark leaves campus.

Wait, except for Tuesdays. Then he leaves earlier. That's right. It had been awhile since he'd tailed the guy. Mark went to rehab.

The Knight dropped his pen and paper on the seat next to him. Then arranged it more orderly and started his car and followed Mark from a distance.

Mark traveled along Riversdale and got on the freeway. The Knight stayed behind the van, ending up at Health Harbor in Warner's Bay. Mark got out of his vehicle and wheeled inside.

Why even bother with the chair? The Knight snorted. Why not just walk inside?

Mark Graham wasn't all he was cracked up to be. The Knight needed to produce evidence to present to Beth. Surely, she'd end her friendship with Mark and run to the Knight.

Even after the Knight had repeatedly warned her, Juanita refused to leave a man in a wheelchair. But no way he'd let Beth slip through his fingers. He had a chance to replay history and control the situation so things worked out according to his plan. Beth and Mark were mere puppets on his stage. And deep down, she wanted him to rescue her from Mark. The Knight would help her understand.

He got back in his car and stared at the outside of

the physical therapy complex. Next week he'd be watching Mark again, only from the inside.

As he drove home, he passed the middle school. Beth had made no mention of his last note. Maybe she hadn't seen it. Should he stop in and visit her room? Perhaps he could leave her a new note. Maybe even send a note directly to her apartment to ensure she received it. A rumble sounded in his stomach. No, he'd do it some other time.

He drove home and stumbled inside his apartment. Better make a sandwich. He walked to the fridge and removed meat, cheese, and mayo, and then headed to the table. He grabbed a loaf of bread from the table and built an impressive ham and Swiss. He opened his lips and lifted the sandwich to his mouth. His watch beeped. He slapped off the alarm and slammed down his snack.

Time to take his meds. Pills did help control the rage, when he decided to take them. He ignored his ham and Swiss and ran his fingers along the outside of the Sig Sauer handgun lying on his table.

Maybe he wanted to feel...something. That's why he'd skipped his medicine every day the past week. Besides, who said he had a disorder? Society. And what did they know?

30

Mark pulled into Fishy Business, shut off the ignition, and sat there lost in thought. After he retrieved the yearbook from the passenger seat of his van, he opened it and stared at his signature, then flipped the page to the note from Rachel he'd read previously.

He moved on to the senior section. That year, the homecoming theme was Home on The Range. He found a picture of Chris and him wearing cowboy hats and standing next to the homecoming float—a covered wagon made from a pickup truck, PVC pipes, and brown poster paper. Good memories.

Then the individual photos of students. He spotted Chris and a few other classmates. Then himself. Whoa. Warmth spread across his face.

Hearts drawn in pencil near his picture and "Mark plus Lizzie" written in the margin. Lizzie—Beth's old nickname. So the note from her friend Rachel about Beth being lucky to get someone's signature—he was that guy.

He shook his head. Though he'd been aware of a few admirers while growing up, Beth had a schoolgirl crush on him, and he'd had no clue. Pretty much managed to ignore her through most of high school. No wonder she was scared to get too close to him.

He remained in his car for a few more minutes. He needed time for everything to sink in. He set the yearbook on the passenger seat and wheeled inside Fishy Business. Bill and Tim stood by the register.

Tim looked at Mark then walked away.

Mark held up his hand. "Wait. Tim, I'm sorry."

Tim turned to face him.

"Beth asked you about Chris, and, well, she's an adult. I'm starting to see that. Sometimes, it's hard to remember we're civilians now, and we're both older. Guess I can't order everyone around like we're still in the military, can I? Anyway, it's not your fault."

"I didn't tell her everything," Tim walked over and placed one hand on Mark's shoulder. "Thought it was best for you to tell her certain things. That is, if you decide you want to. Some stuff might be better left unsaid. Nothing to be gained from it."

Bill looked at the envelope in Mark's hand. "So what's happening now? I see you still have that invitation."

Mark stared into the distance. "An invitation to Thanksgiving dinner with Beth."

Bill nodded. "I know. What are you going to do? You don't have to teach, and the store will be closed. You have no other obligations."

Mark shrugged. "I guess I'm going to eat Thanksgiving dinner with her and her family. Going to see the Martindales." What did God have in store for him?

Tim smiled.

Bill patted Mark on the back. "Good for you."

He examined the envelope again. Red cursive writing. So familiar to something he'd seen before. But what, he wasn't sure. He'd ask Beth about it sometime. If she ever spoke to him again.

๛

Mark shook his head. Marisa must be mistaken. No way Beth was interested in someone like him. Not now at least. Yet, her yearbook confirmed that at one time she did have feelings for him.

Her dinner invitation and homemade buckeye treats were a nice gesture. As a gentleman, he should return the favor. Not to mention it gave him a reason to spend more time with her.

He called her apartment, but she didn't pick up. In a gentle tone, he left a message. "It's Mark. I'm really sorry. Please let me take you out to dinner tonight to make things up to you. I'll stop by around five."

At almost 1700 hours, he wheeled up to her door. He avoided her gaze when she opened it. "Hello."

"Hi. Wait. Just need to turn down my air conditioner. Be right back."

He caught a glimpse of her outfit as she pranced away—a colorful patterned sundress that fit nicely. Her free spirit shone through, even in her choice of attire. And her heels—they added at least an inch or two of height. Had they been standing face-to-face, just about the right level for him to lean over and procure a kiss.

She sauntered outside, locked her door, and then they headed toward his van.

Something else. More makeup than usual. It made her look older. Not the same Beth from years ago. But he wasn't complaining.

He let her control the radio as they drove to the restaurant.

She settled on the local Christian radio station and sang along.

He chuckled inside at her slightly off-key tune. Joining her, Mark added his baritone to the mix. The song ended, and he turned down the volume. "I want to apologize for getting angry with you. You asked Tim a valid question. The problem was I didn't want to hear the story again."

Beth nodded. "You weren't there. I made sure you weren't—out of respect for you."

"You wanted to know what happened to Chris, and I can't stop you from discussing it." He stopped at a traffic light and turned to face her. "I didn't want you to get hurt by what was said, but you're an adult."

She folded her arms. "So you finally got the memo? Good."

"Yeah, I guess I did." He bit back a grin. "I spoke to Marisa—she told me you were working at the mall."

Beth stared out the window. "And you thought I was being immature and irresponsible, wasting money shopping."

"I did, but I was wrong. Do you forgive me?"

"I'll chalk it up as a senior moment." She turned the volume back up then continued singing.

So a little teasing about his age. He'd settle for playfulness over anger.

After a short ride on the freeway, he exited onto a side street and pulled into the palm tree-lined parking lot of Captain Hank's.

Beth pointed to a pink neon sign. "Not Captain Hook's?"

Mark shrugged. "Already taken."

He parked the van.

She reached for the door.

He leaned toward her, touched her left forearm, and took the opportunity to enjoy her floral fragrance.

"Wait."

She furrowed her brows but released her door handle.

Using his ramp, he got out of the van, wheeled to her door, and opened it for her.

She tilted her head. "Thanks? I think."

Good, he'd thrown her off guard a bit. "Did Chris ever tell you about this place?" he asked.

"No."

"I think you'll like it here." Mark led her inside. "This place was built in 1950." Did she care? He ran his hand through his hair. No more trivia.

Captain Hank greeted him. A live parrot adorned his captain's uniform.

"Welcome to Hank's. Enjoy the seafood," the bird squawked.

She turned toward Mark then chuckled. Another good sign. Perfect pink lips framed her stunning smile.

Mark looked at Hank. "Any room out back?"

"Are you kidding? For an old friend, I'd always make room. In fact, I'll make sure you get the best seat in the house."

"Thanks, Hank." He followed his friend outside to the back deck. Beth walked behind them.

Hank pointed to a table in the corner. "This all right for you?"

"Yes, thanks." Mark wheeled toward a chair and pulled one out for Beth.

She began to sit down, then stood and shoved the other chair out of the way before Hank could do so, allowing Mark to scoot his wheelchair next to the table.

Not expected. Now he was off guard.

Hank handed them menus. "I'll leave you alone for a while so you can look over the selection." He winked at Mark. "Take your time."

Good old Hank. Quite the matchmaker.

Beth gripped her menu and perused it.

Mark stuck his hand on it and peeked over the top. "Look down."

Beth scrunched her face. "What?"

He pointed toward the deck. "Under the table. C'mon. Look down."

She cast him a puzzled look then obeyed.

Mark wheeled back a foot then gazed at the small porthole in the deck beneath their table.

"You can see the water below." She smiled, and as best as he could tell, appeared to be having a good time. Mission accomplished.

"That's what he meant by the best seat in the house." He pointed toward the deck railing. "And you have a good view of the waves from here." Mark moved toward the table again.

Beth scooted back to the table, looked at the menu, then set it down. She leaned her head on her hand. "So what do you suggest?"

Could he be back in her good graces that easily?

No one else was around. He'd arrived early on purpose to beat the evening crowd, even talked Hank into opening up a bit early. Waves crashed against the shore. An occasional gull chattered overhead. The flickering candle on the table released a pineapple scent. The perfect evening.

A slight breeze tousled Beth's hair. Her brown eyes sparkled.

She waved her hand in front of him. "Mark?"

"Huh? Oh, right." He shifted his gaze from Beth to his menu. "You like seafood? If so, then I'd suggest the mahi-mahi. If not, the chicken is excellent." He propped up his menu. Hopefully, she hadn't seen his face turn red. If he was as old as she made him out to be, then why'd he feel as giddy as a teenager?

Hank returned to take their orders.

When he left, Beth leaned closer to Mark. "Thanks for the flowers. You didn't sign the card, but I guessed they were from you. By the way, they're lovely."

"Beth, I didn't send you any flowers."

She reached into her purse and withdrew a note. "You mean this isn't from you?"

Mark snatched the note card.

I tried to contact you earlier, but I don't think you got my message. I hope we can still be friends.

"I can see why you'd think it's from me." He made a mental note to give her flowers in the future then turned the card over. "No signature."

"Yeah. It's typed from a florist. Not handwritten. So I don't think it's the Knight."

"Who else has tried to contact you, and more importantly, would be concerned about you remaining friends?"

"I bet it's from Antonio. He probably left me a message. I can check my answering machine when I get home."

"Maybe I need to have a chat with him."

"Whoa. Let me handle this. If he left me a message, I'll call and ask about the flowers."

"What if he denies it?"

"Either way, I'll go to the principal and suggest that maybe the Knight sent it." She sighed. "Guess that means a guard will have to escort me to my car again."

"I'm sorry you have to live like this, but I think it's a good idea. I'm not going to relax until someone catches this guy."

They chit-chatted some more and reminisced about growing up in Beaumont. The talk reminded him of the invitation to spend Thanksgiving with her family. "Please forgive me. I've completely forgotten my manners. Thanks for the buckeyes. They were delicious. And also thanks for the dinner invitation. That was generous of you."

She leaned forward. "So you're coming?"

He nodded. Judging from the look on her face, his response appeared to be the correct one.

"Good. I was hoping maybe you could go grocery shopping with me."

His stomach churned inside. As much as he wanted to enjoy the moment, how could he? Sharing Thanksgiving dinner with her meant interacting with the Martindales, something he'd avoided before. This was about to be an exercise in faith for him.

Mark stared up at the sky. *Well, God.* He shifted his gaze to the ocean. *You made all this. The oceans, the sky. I suppose you have my situation in Your hands, too.* He sighed. Then why did his life feel as if it was careening out of control?

≈∾

Dinner ended, and Beth waved to Hank and the parrot as she and Mark strolled toward his van. Over dinner, Mark mentioned he'd found out about her working at the mall. Did he also know she wasn't dating Antonio?

As they left the restaurant parking lot and headed toward her place, they neared Fishy Business, off on the right. She pointed at the store. "Hey, the lights are on."

"Hmm. Tim and Bill should have left by now."

Dinner was good. Her seafood breath, not so much. Even if Mark didn't notice, she minded. Beth shrugged and removed a stick of gum from her purse. "Maybe someone forgot to turn off the lights."

"Maybe." He pulled into the parking lot. "Hope you don't mind if I run inside and turn them off."

"Want me to come with you?"

"Nah, it'll only take a minute."

"OK." She shoved the stick of gum in her mouth. Minty fresh. Much better.

Mark exited the van and wheeled toward the back of the store.

Beth glanced at her fingernails. They needed painting. Too bad she hadn't noticed before. As she looked beyond them, a red object caught her attention. Sticking out from underneath her seat was a book. She pulled it out. So he carried his yearbook around, too. Odd. She opened it and stared at the signatures. Her insides rumbled but not from hunger. Her yearbook? How had Mark gotten his hands on this? She'd given it to Marisa. And he'd stopped by her place. How much did Mark know about her crush? She was about to find out.

She glanced at the van clock. Mark had been gone for at least ten minutes. Maybe he stopped to use the restroom. Beth grabbed her yearbook and purse and jumped out of the van. She fixed her gaze on the bait store. He'd turned off the lights, but he'd need to leave them on if he was in the bathroom.

She approached the store. "Mark? Hello?" Perhaps he'd gone up front. Even still, some lights should have been on. Craning her head slightly, she peered around the side of building. "Mark?" She walked to the front and tried opening it. Locked. Beth headed around the side of the building and shifted her gaze toward the back of the shop. An overhead security light flickered on and off in the distance. "Hello? Mark?" She jogged closer.

Mark lay on the ground, his wheelchair nearby. She ran to him. "Mark, are you OK? Mark?" Nothing. She crouched down, brushed his blond hair back against his forehead, and set the yearbook next to him. "Don't die on me, too." She willed back tears, attempting to remain calm.

Antonio suspected Mark could walk. Maybe he tried, fell, and then blacked out. She studied his face. Mouth open. His face was bruised. Did he bump into an object as he fell? Or something worse? Chills ran down her spine. The scent of unfamiliar cologne approached. A hand covered her mouth.

"I don't want to hurt you," a male voice whispered. His hot breath blew against her. He yanked her purse from her hand. The yearbook clattered to the ground. "You don't understand how bad I need the money, lady. Gotta get my fix."

She clawed at the man's arms, kicked his legs, and attempted to scream. Not much use. He maintained his hold on her.

Had she finally met up with the Knight? *Dear God, help me.*

As the man tightened his grip, her gaze met Mark's. He'd awakened and fumbled with his phone, probably dialing 9-1-1. Was she the only one who'd noticed? She shifted her gaze to avoid suspicion and continued to claw and kick.

The man turned her around as he held onto her shoulders. He wore a black ski mask. She spit her gum in his face, hoping to throw him off guard.

"I didn't want to have to do this." He drew back his fist and slugged her in the face.

Her head hit the pavement with a dull thud. Her world spun, vision darkening.

≈∞

Mark refused to ride in the ambulance with Beth and chose to drive himself to the hospital. Though he downplayed his fall, once he arrived at the hospital, pain set in.

Bill and Tim met him in the hospital lobby. Bill pushed Mark to the nurse's desk and got him to check in with a doctor. He would have argued, but he was too tired to put up a fight. Tim walked away, presumably to find food.

As soon as the doctor gave his OK and released him, Mark wheeled outside the treatment room and stared at Bill. "Where's Beth? Is she OK? I want to see her."

"She's fine. A small bruise and just a bump on the head. Kid's resilient."

Just a bump? Bottom line, she was hurt. "I can't protect her."

"You did what you could, considering."

"Considering I should be walking, but I'm not. Not good enough. Out of my way." He pushed by Bill and rolled down the hospital corridor toward the nurse's station.

"Where you are going?" Bill asked. "I'm not a relationship expert, but you two need to talk."

"I can't."

"Tim texted me. He's sitting with her. Could be

telling her corny jokes for all we know. You better rescue her."

He shook his head at the clever ploy on his friend's part. *Rescue her.* He might not be able to fend off their attacker, but he could at least save her from Tim's ill attempt at humor. Mark wheeled away from the nurse's counter and down the hall, back the way he'd come. "Show me where they are."

Smiling, Bill maneuvered himself in front then led Mark to the other end of the hospital, but not before they made a slight detour to the gift shop along the way. Good thing they kept late hours and hadn't closed yet.

Bill waved as they approached the waiting room where Tim sat with Beth.

Bill motioned to Tim. "I'm hungry. You?"

"Huh? Oh, uh, yeah." Tim stood and walked toward the cafeteria with Bill.

Mark stowed the gift shop bag in the side pouch on his chair, moved toward Beth, and stared at the ground.

She lifted her head and positioned her face in front of his. "If you have something you need to say to me, at least look at me or something."

"Beth, you don't understand. You're not going to want to hear what I have to say."

She grabbed one of his armrests. "Is this about the wheelchair? Antonio said he saw you walking."

He rubbed his face. "I was in a wheelchair for a while recovering from a shrapnel injury."

"From trying to save Chris. Right, I already know that."

"Yes, but I got better." He pointed to his head. "Now my only injury is up here." The sideways look on Beth's face told him she still wasn't following him. "I have what's called conversion disorder. My condition has been brought on by post-traumatic stress. It's psychosomatic."

Beth's jaw dropped; her eyes widened as she released her hold on his armrest and sunk back into her chair. She sat in silence for a moment then turned to him. "So you really can walk?"

He nodded. "My emotions cause bouts of temporary paralysis."

She bit her lip. "You mean emotions related to Chris and his death?"

"It comes and goes with therapy. I'd had a bad episode right before you came. So when you first showed up, Bill and Tim were concerned I might get worse, but it's the opposite really. I seem to be doing a little bit better." He stared at her. "I'm sorry for not telling you about that. If I had completely worked through it all by now, then maybe I wouldn't be in this thing, and I could have protected you."

"I'm fine."

Mark folded his arms. "You are. But what if something had happened? I wouldn't have been able to live with that."

"I'm OK, but I wish you would have trusted me. It's not like I'm a kid. I'm a grown woman. And I don't appreciate you keeping secrets from me. Though to be fair, you're not the only one with secrets. I have to tell you something. Have to get it out. You won't tell anyone else, will you?"

He shook his head, unfolded his arms, and leaned toward her, all ears. Whatever it was, her secrets couldn't be as dark as his.

"Before your last tour, Chris came home." She

stared in the distance, as if drawing from her memories, then back at him. "I think it was around Thanksgiving."

"Yeah, I came home, too."

"I know." A tear rolled down Beth's check.

He brushed it away.

Her eyes watered more. "I wanted Chris to go the movies with me, but he said he was going with you. He saw you every day in the Marines, and it didn't seem fair. I told him...I yelled at him..." She lowered her voice and choked back a sob. "I told Chris I didn't want to see him again. He stormed out of my room, and that's one of my last memories of my brother." She covered her face with her hands.

He touched her arm. "Chris knew you didn't mean what you said." Mark studied the pale, light green hospital walls. Was it him, or did it smell like death in there? He needed to get outside.

She uncovered her face and rested her arms on the sides of her chair. "I was angry at the time. I shouldn't have said it. And now I can't take it back."

True, he couldn't argue with that. "No, no you can't. But you can ask God to forgive you." Mark laid his hand atop of hers. "And you can forgive yourself."

She stared at the floor. "Not an easy thing to do."

What could he say? It wasn't as if he had it all figured out. Better to change the subject to something that could give her comfort. "So, the police told me while I was being treated that the guy who attacked us and broke into Fishy Business was apprehended."

She straightened her posture. "How'd they catch him?"

"I recognized him."

Beth leaned toward him. "You know him?"

"We've both met him, not that you would have recognized him with the mask. His name is Will Marshall."

"Who's Will?"

"He's friends with Kevin, my teaching assistant. He helped us move things into your apartment. I've seen him on campus with Kevin several times since, and I recognized his voice."

"So he knows where I live?" Beth asked.

Mark nodded. "Also, Kevin mentioned that Will's little brother attends your school. He could have easily gotten those notes to you. I let the police know. They'll want to see those."

"But why would he do this?"

"Who knows?"

"So you think he planned all this out? He's been watching us all along?"

"I don't know, but my teaching assistant apologized for ever introducing us. It's not Kevin's fault, but I know he feels bad. I've taken Kevin fishing several times. He said he'd bragged to Will about my boat and fishing equipment. Kevin suspects Will has a drug problem."

"Now that you mention it, Will did say something about needing a fix."

"So that explains his motive for robbery—to try and fence items to pay for his drug habit. And as for the notes, I guess Will just became infatuated with you." Who wouldn't be? A part of him envied the Knight. At least his feelings for Beth were out in the open.

"So the notes and everything, it's over now?"

Mark rubbed her hand and nodded then let go.

He reached inside the side pouch on his

wheelchair and produced a small teddy bear. "Here. This is for you."

"Thanks."

"It doesn't make up for what happened, but I didn't know what else to do. When you were younger and had tonsillitis, I remember my mom drove me over to your house, and we brought you a teddy bear. It made you smile then, so…"

"It's perfect." She squeezed the bear and grinned.

He released a sigh.

She set the stuffed animal in her lap. "What's the matter?"

"Nothing." He brushed a stray hair behind her ear. "I'm just glad you're safe."

"But something else is bothering you."

Mark folded his arms. "I should have known it was Will. If I had figured things out, then maybe this could have been prevented."

"It's not your fault. You barely know Will. I certainly wouldn't have suspected he'd turn out to be the Knight. And who could have guessed he'd break into the business?"

Speaking of the bait store, he'd been found outside on the ground, with her yearbook and purse nearby. He could understand her purse, but how had the yearbook gotten from the van to there? Perhaps she picked it up and moved it. Maybe she suspected he'd uncovered the identity of her secret crush. Should he bring it up now? No, he'd wait until his upcoming shopping trip with her. A couple hours together would leave nowhere for Beth to run and hide from him. And if that didn't work, they had all of Thanksgiving to discuss things.

31

A week passed—a long, exhausting one. Mark parked near Beth's car outside the grocery store, walked outside his van, and sighed as he grabbed onto a shopping cart for support. He had more physical therapy in his future before his legs gained their full strength. One thought kept him going. He needed to be strong for Beth. Will's arrest helped him relax a little, yet the fear that the Knight could be still on the loose plagued him.

Though Mark had endured a week of intensive therapy and counseling to get this far, there might be future relapses. Still, he'd taken one step further toward conquering his fears and putting the rest behind him, yet new issues lay before him. He planned on spending Thanksgiving with the Martindales. How much did they know? What would they feel inclined to share with their daughter?

He pushed the cart inside the grocery store. Beth stood inside the front entrance, waiting for him.

Hoping to surprise her with his progress, he'd been careful to avoid her over the past week. "Ready to shop 'til you drop?" Did she look at him differently because he could walk?

"I see you've made a bit of progress." She smiled.

"Thanks." He could spill his guts about his progress or what he'd discussed with his psychologist...or wait until later. "Guessing you've never shopped for Thanksgiving dinner before?"

Beth's eyes widened. "That noticeable, eh?"

"I'm guessing that's why you asked for my help."

"I know you helped your mom cook, and I've never hosted Thanksgiving dinner before. I want things to be perfect for my parents."

"You shouldn't underestimate yourself. I've tasted your buckeyes as well as your recreation of my mother's pistachio salad. Not bad. Although I understand wanting things to be perfect. You know, it's just a suggestion, but while you have a one bedroom apartment, I have an entire house to myself—well, Sparky and me. Anyway, we could all eat Thanksgiving dinner at my house, and your parents could stay there, too."

Beth raised an eyebrow. "Are you sure? My dad snores."

Mark chuckled. "I'm well aware. I remember when he'd fall asleep on the couch while Chris and I were watching sporting events. But thanks for the heads up."

Beth removed a can of yams from a nearby shelf and placed them in the cart. "I'm OK with the arrangement as long as you don't mind. I'm sure my parents won't care."

Good move on his part or not—he wasn't sure. Eating with Beth's family was one thing. Having them stay with him was yet another. When Beth would go home each evening, he'd be alone with the Martindales. What if they confronted him about what they knew? He'd overcome a lot lately, but he wasn't sure he was up to such a challenge. Still, if things were to progress between him and Beth, he might have to face the issue.

Did Beth have feelings for him? Was now a good time to bring up the yearbook? He had experience with extracting intelligence. Perhaps he could use his experience to his advantage. "Not to sound ungrateful, but I'm curious as to what made you decide to invite me to your place for Thanksgiving."

Beth held up two packages of dinner rolls and appeared to compare them. "My dad asked me about your plans for Thanksgiving. I was afraid you might say no, but since I need your help cooking, I thought you might feel obligated to come." She chose some rolls and placed them in the shopping cart.

"You don't need me to help you. Maybe you've never cooked Thanksgiving dinner by yourself before, but you could have done it without me."

Beth wrapped a stray hair around her finger. "I know, but it's more fun doing it with someone else."

With someone else. Maybe he *had* gotten closer to the heart of the matter. "By the way, Marisa told me you weren't dating Antonio. I'm sorry I jumped to conclusions. I really was convinced he could have been the Knight, and I didn't want to see you get hurt." That and a touch of jealousy.

"He was a friend. That's all." Beth shook her head. "Even if Antonio had been interested in something more, all he talks about are movies or video games or sports. Kind of annoying."

Mark chuckled. "Really? So the free spirit needs someone more serious in her life?" Interesting.

Beth studied her shopping list. "I thought about what you said about planning ahead, and I want to save up, get my own house, maybe even a dog, get my Master's degree. Who knows?"

Mark wouldn't mind seeing Beth's appointment

book fill up more than a week in advance. Maybe he wasn't the only one changing. "Just remember you can't plan out every minute of your life. What's that verse—a man plans his ways or something, but God guides his steps."

"Yep. Planning ahead's not so bad after all. Guess it means occasionally old people are wise." Beth crooked her finger at him and narrowed her eyes. "But not always, so don't let it go to your head."

He suppressed a smile. "Right." The two of them appeared to be on friendly terms, but how friendly? He didn't like playing games. Sure, there were certain things he must keep from her, that was a given. But he didn't want their feelings for each other to remain hidden.

❧

Almost ten minutes into their shopping trip, Beth caught Mark staring at her.

She lowered a sack of potatoes into the shopping cart and leaned toward him. "Thanks for helping me prepare for Thanksgiving dinner. Everything OK?"

Mark walked beside her and pushed their cart around the produce section. "When you came to Riversdale, I thought I needed to watch out for you, like Chris would. In fact, it felt good to be able to help you."

Beth grabbed a stalk of celery, bagged it, and set it in the cart. "Is that why you're helping me now?" Could that be the only reason? It made sense—helping move furniture, going to the school party with her, taking her to dinner, visiting her at the hospital, even holding her hand for a brief moment. His actions must have resulted from a sense of duty.

"For a while, it seemed like we were having fun, and then not as much." He gripped the handle of the cart. "This shopping trip seemed like a good idea, a chance to—"

Wait, he considered their time together fun? Well, he wasn't the only one. She rubbed the back of her neck. And yet, she wasn't at ease. "Stock up on prune juice and vitamins for seniors?" She clenched her jaw. "Isn't that what guys your age do?"

"You know what I think about the wisecracks?"

She grabbed an onion and examined it. "No, but you're gonna tell me."

His eyes softened. "I think you do it to avoid being serious, to avoid getting close to others."

Why did he care? He certainly had no interest in her beyond the friend level. "Excuse me?"

"You can be serious. I know that because I've seen that side of you, like when we were at the lighthouse. But most of the time, you avoid things that are serious or make you feel uncomfortable."

"Don't we all?" She bagged the onion and dropped it in the cart.

Mark turned toward her. "When we didn't see each other as much, I thought maybe I had done something to upset or offend you."

Why'd he have to be so nice? It'd be easier to put him out of her mind if he'd been rude to her. He'd hurt her once long ago, but even that had been unintentional. Beth released a sigh and shook her head. "No, that wasn't it at all."

Beth glanced at an upcoming shopping display. If she was going to make candied yams, she'd better hurry. "Only one bag of marshmallows left."

She and Mark both reached for it. As her hand rested atop his, her heart raced—nothing to do with the fear of not getting the marshmallows. Beth welcomed the opportunity to study his hand. Strong and warm. At first, she fought the urge to release her grip but then removed her hand. It might be awkward if she continued to hold on.

Mark placed the marshmallows in the cart. "I'm impressed you brought a list. That helps, but maybe next time, we should shop a week in advance so things won't be so picked over."

Next time? Did he assume she'd ask for his help in the future, or was he hoping that, sometime in the future, they'd be doing this together again?

She returned to the produce section and scanned the fruit.

"Looking for something in particular?"

"The right apples." She stepped forward, examined two Granny Smith apples, and placed them in a bag and into the cart.

"What do you plan to do with those?"

"You'll see."

Mark helped her find the remaining items on her list, including treats for Sparky. Afterwards, they drove back to his house to unload the groceries.

After putting everything away and letting Sparky outside to play and enjoy a treat, she walked with Mark toward the living room. He put his arm around her and leaned into her. His balance had improved rapidly, but it was evident he wasn't quite at a hundred percent. Not that she minded his touch.

She settled onto the couch next to him. An acoustic guitar sat propped up next to one side of his coffee table. "Guitar? I didn't know you played. That's awesome." What else didn't she know?

Mark glanced at her. "Do you play anything?"

"The radio." She flashed a smile. "In school, I was into the drama scene rather than band."

"That's right. Chris told me you had a lead in a play."

"Chris told you about that?" Her insides churned.

"Yep. It was always good to get news from home."

"How many other embarrassing details of my life did my brother share with you?" Hopefully nothing related to Valentine's Day from long ago.

Mark chuckled. "Hate to burst your bubble, but he didn't share anything juicy with me. But now I'm curious. Maybe you could share some of these details with me."

"Maybe some other time." Beth got up and headed toward the bathroom. "I'll be right back."

"OK. I think I'll bring Sparky inside."

Beth's cell phone rang just as she was washing her hands. She looked at the display, dried her hands, and took the call right then and there. "Marisa. What's up?"

"How'd the shopping go?"

"Great. The store was full of people, but—"

Marisa lowered her voice. "Do you like him?"

Where did that come from? Beth stared at the mirror, gazing at her reflection. Her eyebrows were arched. "Who? Mark? We're just...friends." Hadn't they been through this before? Besides, he didn't like her.

"You're sure? Because you are having Thanksgiving dinner with him."

Beth noticed a piece of hair that was out of place and fixed it. "Yeah, so he doesn't spend Thanksgiving by himself." Did it matter she was glad they were spending it together?

"Did you know he's read the works of Solzhenitsyn?"

Beth removed her lip balm from her purse and applied it. "Who?"

"Alexander Solzhenitsyn."

"OK…"

"And he's kind of cute, got that whole mysterious way about him and whatnot. I might ask him out for coffee sometime, since you've mentioned you're only friends. But if you like him, I'll back off."

Beth raised her voice. "You like Mark?"

"Yeah. You're OK with that? Right?"

"Yeah." Beth swallowed hard. "Of course."

"Good. Can you text me his number?"

"Now? Sure." She didn't need to have served time in the military to know she was at Threatcon Delta.

❧

Time to extract some intelligence. Mark turned off the TV and held up his phone as Beth entered the living room and joined him and Sparky on the couch. "I got a text message from Marisa. What's that all about?"

"Already? What did she say?"

Judging from the fact her pupils dilated, he'd struck a chord. Still, he wanted to play it cool. "She asked me out for coffee."

Beth played with the ends of her hair. "Huh. Imagine that."

"Did you know about this?"

"I did. And it's just great. She's great, you're great. It's all…great. I'm really…happy." She made a poor attempt at a smile.

Was that a hint of jealousy he detected? He bit back a grin. "You don't sound happy."

Beth shrugged. "It's been a long day, and I'm exhausted from shopping."

"You know, Beth, when Chris died, I was glad I survived. Everyone started talking about how lucky I was, but then there were other times I felt guilty, like it should have been me who died, and Chris should have lived. I was supposed to be happy, but I wasn't."

Beth patted her lap, and Sparky joined her.

Mark sensed he was on the verge of collecting some good intel. He leaned closer to Beth. "So what's the deal?"

"The deal?"

"Why aren't you happy?"

Beth cleared her throat, and Sparky jumped off the couch. "Who me? I'm upset with myself. No one else's problem." Beth grabbed a sports magazine from atop the coffee table and buried her face inside. "But, getting back to you, you should go out for coffee. That's great."

She may have been into drama in high school, but that was the worst acting he'd seen in a while. "I'm glad you feel that way, and Marisa seems nice, but I don't have, um...feelings for her. I want you to know I'll politely decline her request."

"It's OK. I'm fine with the two of you going out."

Perhaps she really didn't care. "Maybe you are, but that's not what I want."

"Right. I understand." She looked up for a second then just that quickly, buried her head in the magazine again. "You're interested in that blonde. Fine."

"Blonde?" He wondered about the source of Beth's

misunderstanding then suppressed the urge to chuckle. "You mean Carol? You thought we were going out?" Mark folded his arms and released a sigh. "So…you're upset with yourself?"

"A little."

"Why?"

She sighed. "Just because."

Mark turned toward her. He pushed the magazine down and away from her face. "Because?"

She turned to face him. "Ugh. Enough with the twenty questions. You want to know why?"

He kept his gaze fixed on her.

She hid her face behind the magazine again. "Because Marisa said how great you are, and I realized she was right. Then when she said she liked you, I was mad at myself for not recognizing how I felt earlier, for not dealing with my emotions. Are you happy now?"

"So…you were mad at yourself for not realizing how you felt earlier. And how do you feel now?"

"Like you're a great friend," she said. "I enjoy spending time together."

"A great friend, eh?" Maybe her schoolgirl crush was a thing of the past.

She placed the magazine on the coffee table and bit her lip. Was she able to read the look of disappointment that surely must have crossed his face? "Yes, but different."

Mark moved his head to maintain eye contact with her. "How so?"

"You think Marisa is nice, but…" She sighed and rubbed her forehead. "Just like I think Tim and Bill are nice, but…"

"They're *just* friends?"

Beth nodded.

He fought to maintain his famous military stare. "Which means we're…more than friends?"

"You're asking me?" Her cheeks reddened.

"Is that how you feel?"

Beth fidgeted with the sofa armrest. "That's what I'd like."

He'd found out what he needed to know—no sense in tormenting her, no sense in making her more flustered, causing her to turn an even darker shade of red. "OK, I wanted you to say it. I started to feel that way too, but then you stopped coming around as much, and when you did, you were with Antonio."

"Because I felt uncomfortable around you. Which is why I couldn't deal with my emotions."

"Uncomfortable? Why?"

"I wasn't sure about what I felt, and I was a little afraid. What if you didn't feel the same way? It was better to hang out with Antonio, because I could keep you at a distance."

"You did a pretty good job. I was confused. But that's in the past. Let's forget about it. And move on."

It took a moment for him to realize where he stood, physically and emotionally—back on his own two feet, about to spend Thanksgiving with the Martindales, and perhaps on the verge of a relationship with Beth Martindale. Was he prepared for these challenges?

Dear God, help me. How can I explain everything to her? I know you've forgiven me. Can Beth do the same?

⤳⤙

After they'd rested and watched some TV, Mark turned off the show and placed one hand on Beth's shoulder. "I was thinking of heading over to the Surfside Coffee Shop? Up for some caffeine?"

"I could use a little." Beth rubbed her eyes. "Are you sure you want to drive all the way over there when you're just going to order it black anyway?"

Mark rose to his feet. "Actually, I want hazelnut."

"Sure you want to be that daring? Shouldn't you stick with plain?"

He caressed the right side of her face. "Pretty sure I know what I want." He fixed his gaze on hers and refused to look away, causing a familiar shade of red to return to her cheeks. "C'mon." He tugged on her hand, and they walked toward his van. Midway there, he stopped and headed back to the house.

"What's wrong?" she asked.

"I forgot something. I'll be right back."

How could he almost forget? Mark hurried inside, grabbed a box, and carried it out it to the van, shielding it so Beth wouldn't see. He placed the box in the back of the van. Minutes later, he pulled into the parking lot of the Surfside Coffee Shop.

He turned toward Beth. "Wait here." He went to the back of the van and removed the contents of the box then returned to the driver's seat. "These are for you." He handed Beth a bouquet of colorful flowers. "I felt bad the police confiscated your other flowers as evidence." Not to mention he really wanted to buy her some.

Beth leaned over the flowers and sniffed the bouquet. "These are lovely. And much better because they didn't come from the Knight."

Mark got out of the van, met Beth by her door, and opened it for her. He scanned the nearly empty parking lot illuminated only by the remaining pink and purple glow of the setting sun and a blinking overhead street light that needed changing.

Beth looked into his eyes. "Are you OK?"

"Am I OK? Almost." Mark reached over and cupped her chin then drew her head forward. Beth closed her eyes, and Mark leaned in closer, taking in her floral scent, and kissed her. A cherry taste lingered in his mouth.

"I—" Beth cleared her throat. "I wasn't expecting that."

"Oh?" Maybe he shouldn't have done that. "Too forward, too soon?"

Beth lifted her finger up to his mouth to shush him. "I didn't expect it, but that doesn't mean I didn't like it." She leaned in and released a gentle sigh. Again they kissed, only this time longer.

Blushing, Beth gazed at the ground and kicked at the gravel with her shoes.

"I have to tell you. I saw your yearbook at Marisa's, and I borrowed it. You said it wasn't from my senior year, yet it appears you were wrong." He tipped her chin toward him. "But something tells me you already knew that."

"You looked at it?"

"Of course. I had to find out what words of wisdom I'd written to you. 'Have a nice summer.'"

"Don't forget the smiley face."

He brushed a stray hair behind her right ear. "So that really meant something to you?"

"You hung out with my family. I saw you when I cheered for football games. And you sang in the school play. I couldn't wait to be in one of the high school dramas. And I guess when you wrote that, my little naïve, junior high mind took it to mean something more. Later I realized you were only being friendly, and by then, I was crushed."

She'd hung onto his words all those years. "To be fair, you were in middle school."

"I know."

"Well, I'd be happy to sign all your yearbooks now."

"Yeah, I'm sure you would." Playfully, Beth slugged him in the arm as they entered the coffee shop.

Once inside, Mark ordered for them. Hazelnut for himself and a minty mocha concoction for Beth. As they sat at the corner table, he surveyed the establishment. The place appeared deserted, likely because of the impending holiday.

Beth stood. "I'm getting sugar. Do you want any creamer or sweetener?"

Mark gripped his coffee. "It doesn't need that other stuff to dress it up. I like it the way it is." He looked at her, grinned, and took a sip. "Thanks."

After adding sugar to her coffee, Beth sat next to him and sipped in silence.

"So what if I'd said I wanted to go out with Marisa?" he asked.

"Then I would have been happy for Marisa and you. You're my friends. That's what friends do."

"Laying down your life for your friend?"

"What I did hardly compares to what you did for Chris. You were willing to risk your life to save him."

He rubbed his forehead. If she only knew the half of it. Good thing she didn't. "Perhaps, but you were willing to lay aside your desires, your feelings, for your friend." Mark glanced at her. "I think that's pretty noble."

"Thanks." Beth sipped her coffee. "Do you ever

wonder…?"

"What Chris would think? Yes, I've thought about it. But then I also thought if he hadn't died, then none of this would have happened. I mean, if he had stayed at home, you probably would have stayed at home, or he and I would have run the bait store." He'd lost Chris, but God also had brought Beth into his life. It was funny how things had worked out.

"And then he would have helped me with my flat tire and not you. You know, I don't believe in coincidence. God must have planned it. Maybe we can look at this as something good that came from Chris's death."

Yes, it was a good thing. His shoulders tensed. The only one.

Beth rummaged through her purse then removed a pen. "I have a great idea for a lesson plan. Figured I better write it down before I forget." Beth scribbled on a napkin.

A lesson plan idea out of the blue. Maybe that was how the mind of a free spirit worked. He studied her letters—swirly cursive. "Nice writing."

He pulled out the envelope that had contained his invitation to spend Thanksgiving with her. "I guess I must have remembered your writing from Fishy Business or from your letters to Chris."

"What do you mean?"

"Well, when I saw the envelope for your Thanksgiving dinner invitation, the writing looked familiar."

"Oh?" She blushed and avoided eye contact.

Mark waved the envelope in front of her. "Beth, is there another reason why I recognize the writing?"

"Perhaps." She folded her arms and leaned over

the napkin.

"Care to tell me?"

"Not really."

"I'm sorry you feel like you can't confide in me."

"I would, but it's—"

The door chimed, and a middle-aged man walked in the café.

Mark studied his cup and leaned closer to Beth. "You'd tell me but... It's too hurtful? Too sad?"

"Try embarrassing."

"Worse than the yearbook?" Now he'd done it. Her face turned bright red. Oh, boy. "Look, whatever it is, was probably so long ago, I'm sure we'll look back on it and laugh."

Beth hung her head. "I don't know about that."

"How bad can it be?" Surely, it wasn't like his secrets. Still, what right did he have to ask her to share hers? None whatsoever.

She held up her coffee cup and admired it. "February fourteenth, my eighth-grade year. You were a senior. The cheerleaders made candy-filled mugs for different football players. I was stoked because I had your name."

He tried hard to suppress the nervous laughter— just the thought of her being excited because she had his name. Still, he had to consider her feelings. *Maintain a serious look.*

"So I wrote you this note and attached it to the mug. Chris got a note from one of the senior girls, and you, all you received was a note from the little Martindale. I guess you were pretty embarrassed. So after school, when you stopped by my house with my brother, you handed me back the mug and basically thanked me but suggested I give it to a boy closer to my age. I hated Valentine's Day for a long time and didn't like my brother hanging out with you afterward. I wasn't exactly excited to see you when I first arrived in Riversdale either, but that changed. Anyway, that could be why you remember the writing."

"I'm sorry. But you were only in eighth grade. I was a senior. Wait. Is that the reason for all the elderly jokes?"

"I was too young for you. Not good enough. I was Chris's little sister, nothing more. And then, years later, you came back to town, saw me in front of the café, and you didn't even say as much as hello. That's not the only time. You came to Chris's funeral. I saw you sitting off to the side." She buried her head in her hands for a moment and then looked up again. "Mark, for so long, I've felt… invisible. Maybe what happened in the past meant nothing to you, but it broke my heart."

He moved closer and took her hand. "I'm sorry about what happened. I can't change the past. But I hope to make sure I never break your heart again."

Whoa. Where did those words come from?—things he shouldn't have said, shouldn't have promised, especially with something so big he was still keeping from her, and intended to keep from her forever. But on the off chance she did find out, he would indeed break her heart. No doubt about it. But the words were already out there. He could only hope and pray she'd never uncover this one last secret. He hated keeping things from her, but this was for her own good.

32

Since Mark left his house early in the morning, no one else had entered or exited for several hours. The Knight was sure of it, and after watching the house from a distance for a period of hours, he ought to know. He studied dates, times, and other pertinent information in his notebook. Today was the housekeeper's day off.

After running his fingers through his newly dyed hair, he closed his car door and sauntered over to Mark's front door. The Knight listened, but no noise came from inside. Once he opened the unlocked door, a little black creature scampered outside. He grabbed the dog's collar and scooped it up. The animal barked with intensity and flashed his fangs. The animal would make too much noise and give him away. The Knight clamped his hand over its muzzle and jogged to his car. The dog wrestled in his grip. No one else appeared to be outside. The Knight shoved the dog into his vehicle and took off, parking one block away.

The dog continued barking. The Knight reached for his Sig Sauer and pointed at the animal. It tilted its head. *Dumb, cute, furry little thing.* Besides, the Knight hadn't brought a silencer. Someone might hear something, not to mention he didn't want to mess up his car. He eyed the bottle of hand sanitizer that sat in his center console. Once the dog was gone, he'd need to wipe the car clean. Never telling what germs dogs might carry. Supposedly clean animals—yeah right. He willed himself not to scratch the prominent temporary tattoos that adorned his arm and neck. Probably would infect his skin with some canine disease.

After he put away the gun, he drove to a burger joint around the corner. He ordered a cheeseburger and fed it to the dog. When the animal finished its snack, the Knight scooped it up and walked back toward Mark's house. He'd come back later for what he wanted and chalk today up to reconnaissance.

Mark's housekeeper stood near the front door. "Sparky! Where are you?"

The woman wasn't even supposed to be there today. Now what? The Knight walked through Mark's yard, carrying the dog.

The housekeeper met him halfway. "You've found him. You found Sparky. I don't know how he got out. Thank you. Thank you."

The Knight handed the woman the dog.

"Come inside." She opened the door. "I'll be right back. Let me put him outside."

While in the foyer, the Knight got enough of a glimpse to notice Mark's wheelchair inside the house—without him in it. He gritted his teeth. Just as deceitful as his stepdad. Which meant Mark was just as dangerous.

The housekeeper returned. "May I have your name? I'm sure Mr. Graham would be happy to know you found his dog."

The man extended his hand to her and grinned. "Knight, Mr. Knight."

She shook it. "Nigh-yeet," she sounded. "OK, Mr. Nighyeet, I will let him know. Thank you. You live close by? Mr. Graham might like to have you over for coffee or something."

The Knight licked his lips. "I think I'd like that."

33

Mark waited until seven forty-five to pick up Beth at her apartment and then drove them to Fishy Business. After unlocking the store and turning the front sign to read 'Open,' he walked over to the cooler, removed two sodas, and handed one to Beth. "Thanks for spending the day with me. You didn't have to help out."

"I'm caught up on my grading, and I don't need to work at the mall until the day after Thanksgiving. Besides, I think it's nice you offered to work today so Tim and Bill could spend time with their family."

He stuffed his hands in his pockets. "Your parents aren't coming in until this evening, so I didn't mind."

"And we get to spend more time together, so you won't hear me complaining." Beth took a few sips of her soda then rubbed her arms.

Mark pointed to a backpack next to the desk at the back of the store. "If you unzip my bag, there's a sweatshirt inside, in case you're cold."

"Thanks." Beth unzipped the bag, removed the sweatshirt, and pulled it over her t-shirt. "A little big but it works."

Mark reclined on a stool near the register and envisioned their chance meeting in front of the café over ten years prior. The shy teen he'd avoided back then was the stunning woman beside him. "I know you won't believe me, but I think it looks nice on you."

Her shoulders slumped, and he grabbed her hand. "You OK?"

"You were right. I crack jokes to keep people at a distance. So, now, getting close to someone…someone I care about" —Beth cleared her throat—"that scares me a little."

"And it's easier to keep your distance so you don't have to worry about losing them." Of all people, Beth ought to realize he understood how she felt.

"Right."

"There's no fear in love. God loves us and doesn't want us to be afraid. As *someone* reminded me, we have to trust God."

Beth studied their interlaced hands and smiled. "Sounds like a wise person."

He turned to face her, and using both hands, attempted to infuse warmth into hers. "Look, are you sure us spending Thanksgiving together is OK? I can go hang out with Bill and Tim if it's not."

"I'm sure it's OK. Though I might need to pinch myself as a reminder this is real." She smiled.

"How about a kiss instead?" Sitting on the stool narrowed the height gap between them. He tugged her close. Their lips brushed then connected. Reluctantly, he pulled away. The part of him that didn't want to let go lost out against the part of him that knew they should take things slow.

Beth grinned and walked away with a box of lures. "I'll put these away for you."

Mark set his Bible on the counter next to the register. The day before Thanksgiving, there shouldn't be too many customers. A good time to catch up on reading the Word. Not to mention a good distraction from Beth for the moment.

The door chimed, and a familiar-looking man charged toward him.

"Private Davis?" Mark smiled and waved. "Kent, it's been a long time." Mark extended his arm and shook hands with the man.

"It has, hasn't it?"

Mark folded his arms. "What brings you here?"

"I've been working at an orphanage not far from here, over the border in Mexico. I can't get home for the holiday, so Bill and Tim invited me to their house."

"They were going to work today, but I decided to come in so they took the day off."

"It's good to see you. It's been a long time. I think the last time I saw you was the night Chris died."

"Yep. I was in the infirmary for a long time afterwards."

Kent's eyes widened then he fingered the Bible beside the register. "That's right. And while you were in there, I was reassigned. Good to see you still seeking God's truths."

Mark nodded. Kent had led him to the Lord. Could he have possibly..."Kent, did Chris ever talk to you about God?"

"Actually, the night before Chris was killed, he came to me. He said you'd been talking to him about the Bible. He wanted to pray to receive Christ, but I think he needed to talk to someone other than you. He accepted Christ late in the night before you left for your mission."

Mark shook his head and stared at Kent. "Why didn't he say anything to me?"

Kent looked at the ground. "I don't think he had time."

Mark placed his hand on Kent's shoulder. "I

appreciate you sharing that. I've been carrying around these feelings about Chris's death, but your news helps me feel"—he took a deep breath and willed himself not to cry—"more at peace." That wasn't a lie. Even though it didn't wipe away all the guilt and secrets, it did help.

Beth's hand rested on his shoulder. "Me, too," her voice quivered. "We've got to tell my mom and dad. They'll"—She cleared her throat—"want to know." She held out her hand to Kent. "I'm Beth Martindale. Chris's sister."

Kent smiled. "Chris always said that when you grew up you'd be a knockout. It's good to meet you, Beth. Your brother—he was a good man." He nodded toward Mark. "Good to see you again." Kent waved. "You have a good Thanksgiving."

"You, too." Mark inhaled another deep breath and relaxed his shoulders.

Mark's cell phone vibrated. If it was a call, he'd return it later. If it was a message, he could read it some other time. He couldn't imagine anything so important as to command his attention at that moment.

34

The Knight consumed half a pill with his Thanksgiving breakfast. Just enough to help him summon the courage to call his beloved Beth but not so much so to quench his desire to rescue her from the likes of scoundrels such as Mark Graham. So hard to contain his enthusiasm. Not the same as conversing with his lady fair face-to-face but exhilarating nonetheless. At least she would hear his voice.

He wouldn't stay on long to avoid allowing Riversdale PD the opportunity to trace the call. And he was smart enough to use a prepaid cell phone. One he'd toss afterward. So no concerns about the conversation being traced back to him. Pleasing and irritating at the same time. If society wasn't so backward, they'd understand his motives. Then there would be no reason to stay in hiding, no need to contact Beth in secret.

While waiting for the pill to take full effect, the Knight entered his shrine to Beth and lit the candles surrounding her photo. He grabbed a paper from his table—a printout from the faculty page of Riversdale Community College's website. After he tore the paper in two, the Knight proceeded to burn Mark Graham's image. When finished, the Knight approached Beth's photo. "It's OK. I'm here to rescue you. I'm your Knight. Worry no more, my fair maiden. Soon, you will be free. Mark Graham will no longer hurt you.

And you and I will be together. The way it should be."

Confident his pills had kicked in, the Knight turned on the prepaid cell phone and dialed Beth's number. Poor helpless girl. Didn't even know to make her number unlisted. He'd have to instruct her on the finer points of safety once they were together. His heart raced with each ring of the phone.

"Hello?" Beth answered.

The Knight gripped the arm of his couch. Words were not coming as he'd hoped. But he'd planned ahead. On the coffee table sat a CD player. The Knight played the song he'd chosen for Beth. As a ballad of friendship and love played in the background, the Knight closed his eyes and sat in meditation.

"Hello? Who is this?" Beth asked then hung up the phone.

"Noooo." The Knight snorted and knocked his palm to his forehead. "Oh sure, I can talk to her now." He tossed his pills across the room. "Worthless medication. Never helps me do what *I* want to do."

Pills did nothing but turn him into a quiet, repressed man. Nice for those concerned with following society's norms but clearly not for him.

35

Again, Mark glanced out his living room window. Even Sparky, who sat atop a chair and was able to look out the window, appeared to be anticipating Beth's arrival. He'd heard Beth's parents moving around in the guest room earlier, but they hadn't joined him yet. While waiting for Beth, Mark retrieved his cell from his pocket and glanced at the screen—a text message from Lupe from earlier:

SPARKY RAN AWAY TODAY, BUT MR. NAYEET FOUND HIM.

Mr. Nayeet? Never heard of him. Maybe Nayeet was the new neighbor around the corner. He should stop by the man's place sometime. He could thank him for returning the dog and invite the man over for dinner or coffee. Perhaps Beth could join them.

As Beth pulled into the driveway, Mark's shoulders relaxed.

Beth walked inside, mascara smudged around her red, swollen eyes.

Mark hugged her, and her body shook. "Are you all right?"

"Not really. I received a prank call this morning. I picked up the phone, but no one answered. Only breathing on the other end followed by some music."

He gripped her shoulders. "What kind of music?"

"Some cheesy folk song. I figured it was a student

and wasn't going to worry about it because the Knight was behind bars. Then, as I'm about to leave my house, I got a call from the Riversdale Police Department. They're not so sure Will sent me those notes. A handwriting expert took samples of his writing and doesn't believe that it matches the notes from the Knight. So I told the police about the phone call. Unfortunately, they can't trace it now."

"But the police have the flowers from Antonio."

"We can't know that he sent them. They said they couldn't trace the flowers back to any florists in the area, and they didn't find any fingerprints or DNA on them or the note that came with them. So even if Antonio did send them, we can't prove it."

Mark wrapped his arms around her, and Beth nestled her head onto his shoulder. "It's going to be OK. If you want, Bill and Tim could pick you up from work each day. I'm sure your principal will have a security guard escorting you again. Maybe try to avoid Antonio, just in case. Your friend Marisa might let you stay with her if you'd like." His grip tightened. "And you know I'm not going to let you far from my side." He stared at the ceiling. He'd failed to save Chris. What made him think he could protect Beth? He kept a firearm at work only as a safety precaution. Perhaps he should keep it with him at all times from now on. Since he'd left the military, he'd feared keeping one. Could he trust himself and his emotions? He wasn't sure.

"First thing tomorrow, I'll call the principal and tell him that the police think they haven't caught the Knight. But for now, there's not much more we can do. It's Thanksgiving." She grabbed a tissue from the box on the coffee table and wiped her eyes. "I don't want my parents to see me like this." She sniffed and laughed. "And I really don't want you to see me like this. I'll be right back." Beth hurried off to the bathroom.

When she returned, her eyes appeared less puffy, and she'd removed the mascara smudges.

Beth joined Mrs. Martindale on the couch and hugged her. "Hi, Mom."

For Mark, it was as if watching from a distance. This wasn't his family. Maybe he shouldn't be there. For a moment, he considered what it would have been like if his mom were still alive.

He remembered Chris saying he helped his dad carve the turkey. Perhaps Mr. Martindale would ask him to help.

Mark reclined in his chair, unsure of how much they knew but confident he could find out by gauging their reaction as they interacted with him.

Mr. Martindale rubbed his eyes. His hands were wrinkled and appeared frail. Time had flown. He should have reconnected with them sooner. The Martindales appeared friendly, but then again, these were the kind of people who could forgive anything.

Mr. Martindale smiled. "How fortunate you live so close to Beth. She told me you fixed her flat tire. And then when that man attacked her..."

Mark's shoulders tensed. The attack remained a little too fresh in his mind.

Mrs. Martindale smiled at Mark. The ceiling light accentuated the sheen of her silvery hair. "Divine intervention, I tell you. I asked God to watch over her."

"She's so far away," Mr. Martindale said. "It's nice to know she has a friend nearby."

"Beth has her own place, two jobs." Mark made brief eye contact with Beth. "She's doing all right without me, sir."

Mr. Martindale adjusted his glasses. "Still, it's nice to have a friend around."

"That's true." He shifted his gaze to the dining room. Four settings were arranged around the table. Today, Chris should have been at one of them. Instead, he lay six feet under. Was it too late to duck out the back of the house and run away?

Mr. Martindale tilted his head. "How long has it been since you've been to Beaumont?"

Mark glanced at Beth. Would she bring up the time they'd met outside the Hometown Café—the time when he didn't have enough courage to face the Martindales? He pursed his lips. "Too long. Far too long."

Mr. Martindale looked serious for a moment and nodded. "I agree. So what are you up to these days?"

Mark ran his hand through his hair. "I teach History of Civilization at the local community college, and a couple of my buddies and I own a bait and tackle store."

"Oh, Beth told me that. Great."

Beth went to her dad and grabbed him by the arm. "Dad, I don't mean to interrupt you, but we have some news we need to share. Yesterday, we ran into Kent Davis. He served with Mark and Chris."

Mark looked at Mr. Martindale. "Kent later became a pastor—"

Mr. Martindale nodded. "Right, I remember."

Beth stared at the ground. "He said that..." She bit her lip. "He said he talked to Chris the night..."

Mark leaned closer to Mr. Martindale. "What Beth is trying to say is Kent was able to discuss the Gospel with Chris before he died. Chris had become a

Christian. Both of us, and I'm sure, both of you, shared God with Chris. And I don't think any of us knew he had accepted Christ before he died."

Mrs. Martindale smiled but her lip trembled. She clasped her hand over her mouth for a moment. "That's very comforting. Thank you so much for telling us."

Mr. Martindale teared up.

Was the man going to cry? Mark couldn't stand the sight of it. At least they hadn't gone into detail about that night—probably the only thing holding him back from having another episode right now.

Mr. Martindale rubbed his eye. "So when did you become a Christian?"

Mark scratched his head. "In the Marine Corp, about six months before Chris's death."

Beth put her hand on her mother's shoulder. "There's more."

"More?" Mrs. Martindale asked.

Beth locked eyes with her mom. "Mark would never bring this up on his own, but I will." She made eye contact with her dad. "Mark was injured trying to save Chris."

Mark closed his eyes. He didn't ask for recognition. If it weren't for Kent's good news, he'd rather avoid discussing Chris's death altogether.

The Martindales wrapped their arms around him.

He hadn't saved their son. Why were they hugging him?

"Thank you," Mrs. Martindale said.

Mark shrugged. "By trying to save him...I didn't do anything special, just what anyone would have done, what Chris would have done." Moistness on his face—he quickly brushed it aside. Marines didn't cry.

Hopefully, no one noticed. *Uh oh.* He caught Beth staring at him.

Beth looked away. "Mom, would you like to help me with some of the side dishes?" She grabbed her mom by the arm and walked toward the kitchen.

Mrs. Martindale sighed. "This has been quite a Thanksgiving."

Sure he had tried to save Chris, but Mark was no hero. Far from it.

Considering he was the king of trivia, what did he know about sinkholes, and what was the probability one might suck him in right now? Maybe he could pray for one.

❧❦

Mark sat with Mr. Martindale on the couch and watched a Thanksgiving Day parade: first a marching band, then some clowns, and later a drill team twirling their batons. For years he'd joined the man in the same living room with Chris to watch TV, but with the tables turned—the Martindales in *his* house—Mark didn't experience the same level of comfort. Shame and guilt racked him. There was the Mark they once knew, and the one he'd kept from them. Living a dual life was almost more than he could bear.

During a commercial, Mr. Martindale turned toward Mark and smiled. "We're so happy to spend Thanksgiving with you. I overheard Debbie say she gave Beth your mom's recipe for apple pie, and they plan on making you one."

"They didn't have to do that. It's only me, same old kid from the other end of town." Same kid—who was he kidding? Then again, he did miss Mom's pie.

The parade resumed, and Mr. Martindale turned down the volume. "We appreciate you looking after our daughter."

"Not a problem. In some ways, Beth's a little like Chris." Mark bit back a grin. "A little impulsive. Although she'd probably argue she only has his good qualities."

"That sounds about right. I want you to know we don't feel Chris's death was your fault. You did what you could to try to save him." Mr. Martindale ran his hand over his chin. "For a while, Deb and I blamed ourselves because we didn't become Christians until he was in the Marines, and we felt badly that we hadn't taken Chris to church more when he was younger. But once we got saved, we prayed for him, and for Beth, and for you."

"Prayed for me, really?"

Mr. Martindale grinned. "You'll always have a special place within our family."

"About that, sir..." Good thing he'd worn extra deodorant. His only hope in the battle against perspiration. Because anticipation of his next words with Mr. Martindale caused his sweat glands to go into overdrive.

Mr. Martindale steepled his fingers. "Please, call me Jim."

"Sir, I'm not sure I can do that, but I appreciate that you consider me a part of your family. I'm grateful for the kindness you've shown over the years, and I would never want to do anything to hurt your family." What should he say next? He still wasn't sure what they knew.

"We understand."

Mark stared at the floor. "Good, sir. Because while

we're on the topic of family, I'd like to ask for permission to date your daughter. But I also don't want to cause any problems."

Mr. Martindale chuckled. "She's twenty-six. You're what, in your early thirties now? You don't need my permission."

"No, sir. But I'd still like to make sure it's OK with you."

"I appreciate your respect for our family. And if anything, I'd feel better knowing she has you around. California seems so far away. But you have to let your kids go, and so we did." Mr. Martindale wiped his eyes and composed himself. "Goodness, you'd be watching over my daughter. What do I owe you?" Mr. Martindale managed a smile.

"Funny, sir." And yet with the Knight on the loose, the man's words didn't seem quite so humorous.

Mr. Martindale appeared to have taken it well. After all, he hadn't given Mark his famous, menacing stare.

Mark leaned toward Mr. Martindale. "You know, I'm sure Beth has some time off around Christmas. Maybe we can try to visit Beaumont then."

Mr. Martindale wiped his eyes again. "That would be great."

"You should be proud, sir. She's saving her money. You taught her well."

Could he meet a nicer family than this? His insides churned. *God, please help me. I have to talk to someone. I can't live like this. Show me what to do.*

36

The Knight remembered his encounter with Mark Graham's housekeeper and snickered at the hint of an invitation to meet his rival.

He was sitting at his dining room table drinking coffee when the morning edition of the *Riversdale Herald* arrived. Taking a bite of scrambled eggs, he read the first two stories—one about beach erosion control and the other on the Riversdale Thanksgiving parade. So far, nothing exciting. The next article caught his attention. He dropped his fork, clanging it against his plate.

According to the article, the Riversdale PD planned to reopen the cold case involving the murder of Juanita Gonzalez. No weapon had been found. But what if that'd changed? The police might have the murder weapon or DNA evidence. The Knight rubbed the back of his neck. Or both—DNA and a weapon.

In that case, he would need to lie low for a while. But how could he continue to look after Beth? He walked toward the shrine and knelt in front of her picture. Flames from the ring of crimson candles danced. He leaned forward, careful not to set his arm on fire, and touched Beth's photo. Maybe there were other ways of ensuring her safety, like watching her from a distance. It shouldn't be too hard to install a webcam in her classroom. Before heading to the bedroom to pack his things, he shot a final look at the photo. *I've got my eyes on you.*

He retrieved a picture of Juanita from his bedroom and hugged it to his chest. Though the Knight could watch Beth from the webcam, he couldn't risk visiting Juanita's grave. Though only six feet above and ten minutes away from Riversdale Cemetery, the photo would have to serve as his only connection to his dead friend for now. He hated the man who stole Juanita's heart—a man in a wheelchair, like Mark had been. But Mark could walk. The Knight tightened his grip on the picture frame. Mark was a fraud, just like the Knight's stepdad.

The Knight placed Juanita's photo on his dresser and returned to the dining table. He turned the page of the newspaper and read about the attack on Beth. In the face of danger, Mark had failed to protect her. The Knight grunted. Completely unsatisfactory.

So much to be done, yet now was the time to stay hidden. He didn't want to rot in jail for Juanita's murder. Especially since her killing had been justified.

37

Returning from an afternoon fishing trip, Mark entered Fishy Business from the back, Beth by his side. He set down a cooler, removed two small striped bass, and placed them in the freezer. Either he needed a larger deep freeze or he needed to release more fish instead of bringing them back to the store.

Beth leaned her head on his shoulder. They'd fished for several hours. She had to be tired.

He interlaced his fingers with hers. How tiny they were next to his. Hard to believe they'd been dating for two weeks...two weeks since their first kiss. Perhaps he should have stolen one before they came inside the store.

Tim grinned and pointed. "Hey, look, it's Mark and the Mrs."

Bill glared at his brother.

And a good thing, too. If Beth hadn't been around, Mark would have done the same and then some. So maybe he and Beth finished each other's sentences. It didn't bother him. Everyone else, well, they could adjust. Truth be told, he had no problem with Beth becoming "Mrs. Graham," but that didn't mean Tim had to give him a hard time about it.

The doorbell chimed, and a man dressed in a gray uniform walked inside and over to the cooler. He appeared to be taking inventory on a clipboard.

Beth stepped closer to get a better look. "You got a

new vendor?"

"Yeah, we don't know what happened," Tim said, "but it doesn't matter."

Bill shook his head. "One day Randy was gone, and then the other guy came."

Beth folded her arms. "That seems to happen a lot."

"What do you mean?" Mark asked.

"Remember Antonio?"

Mark put his arm around her and walked outside the store. "Antonio? Tall, thin, couldn't keep his eyes off of you? Nope, never heard of him."

She held his hand. "Anyway, he broke his teaching contract midyear, just left his job. Very odd. Some sort of personal business."

"So he won't be at school with you every day?" He released a breath he didn't know he'd been holding. While Will Marshall had been the man who attacked them that night, he'd been cleared of writing notes to Beth, and the real author was never found. Mark had continued to suspect Antonio, even though she hadn't received any more notes. Who else had such easy access to Beth's classroom?

He leaned in and gave her a short kiss—way too short.

Beth glanced back at the store. "Tim referred to me as the 'Mrs.' What's that all about? Am I spending too much time with you? Do I need to give you space, more time to hang out with the guys?"

He liked his friends, but these days, he'd much rather spend time with Beth. And if that didn't spell love, he didn't know what did.

"No, it's only Tim"—he released a sigh—"being Tim. Don't worry about it." The joy of working with friends.

"OK, then I won't. You don't have to tell me twice." Beth looked at her watch. "I better go, or I'll be late for the school district meeting. I heard it's supposed to be important. I'm hoping it won't take all day, so let's still plan on having dinner together."

He kissed her forehead then moved to her lips.

"OK, OK." She chuckled. "I'll see you later." Beth walked away then waved as she got into her car.

Mark marched back inside, over to where Tim stood, and flashed him his infamous look. "The Mrs.?" He liked Tim well enough, but there was a reason he chose to confide more in Bill.

38

The Knight lounged on his plastic-covered sofa and removed sweat from his neck and back using hand wipes. The good-for-nothing landlord said he'd fix the malfunctioning heater as soon as possible. The Knight paused to consider how easily he could push the landlord from the top of the balcony stairs and make it look like an accident. Just one nudge—one good push. The Knight flinched, realizing he'd have to touch the man. Many women entered and exited the super's apartment on a daily basis. The Knight could only imagine what diseases the man might carry. But hey, that's what gloves were for. Besides, the way that man treated women, he'd only get what he deserved. The Knight shook his head. So many women out there who needed his help and not enough hours in the day to rescue them all. Too bad he couldn't clone himself. The phone rang twice before he answered it. "Hello?"

"This is Detective Mullins from the Riversdale Police Department." Once the officer on the phone confirmed to whom he was speaking, he continued, "You were friends with Juanita Martinez. We'd like to call you back in for questioning."

Using a fresh wipe, the Knight removed sweat from his forehead. "Oh? I already gave you a statement. What happened to that?"

"We're calling back all witnesses in hopes of shedding more light on the case. You were a friend of hers. Wouldn't you like to help solve her murder?"

As much as he wanted to point out to this dolt that Juanita's death wasn't really a mystery, the Knight decided to play along. Prison was not the place for him. If only the Riversdale Police Department would do their job and keep the real criminals behind bars—guys like Mark who would only end up hurting Beth. Or scum like his landlord. "Of course. I'll do anything I can to help."

"Can you meet me at the station in an hour?"

"That's short notice, but I suppose I can make it."

"Good, I'll see you then." As much as he wanted to run, he doubted he could throw together a plan to take Beth with him. And he wasn't about to leave town without her. Sure, he could still watch her from the webcam, but leaving her alone with Mark and no one close by to watch over her—it wasn't the knightly thing to do.

He snatched his medicine from the coffee table. Should he take the pills or not? On one hand, they helped him remain calm. On the other, what if he became calm enough that he told what happened? While he believed Juanita's death was justified, the Riversdale PD wouldn't see it from his point of view.

Gripping the pill bottle, he made his decision and popped two caplets. The drive to the police station proved to be enough time for the medicine to perform its magic. Once inside a detective's office, the Knight felt at ease, what society referred to as sane or normal. The detective led him into a small room with a glass window, instructed him to take a seat behind a table, and left the room for a moment. Probably watching him from the other side of the window. Maybe waiting to see if he'd flip out and lose control. Good thing he'd taken his meds. Otherwise, the walls of the small room would be closing in on him right about now.

The detective entered the room and sat across from the Knight. "Is it too cold in here? I can get you some coffee, if you'd like."

"No, no." Who knows who might have touched the beverage? Though his pills prevented him from freaking out over the germs in the room, the Knight still made a mental note to shower once he got home. "I'm fine. I'd really rather get this over with."

"Oh, are you in a hurry to get somewhere?"

"No, I…came here to help you, and that's what I want to do."

"Good. In an earlier statement, you mentioned you were friends with Juanita. You'd met her at work."

The Knight crossed his legs. "That's correct."

"And did you purchase a burial plot for her?"

Something new. Something the police hadn't asked about before. "Yes." That was all they had? They couldn't have asked him this over the phone?

The detective crossed his arms. "Why?"

"Why not? Juanita was a good friend. And seeing as she didn't have much money and no family in the area, I decided to ensure she received a proper burial."

"Fair enough. Before you leave today, we'd like to take a DNA sample. Only a cheek swab. Shouldn't hurt a bit."

The Knight scratched his head. The police said they had new evidence. Was it possible they found his DNA? As meticulous and careful as he'd been to wear gloves before and after the murder, he doubted they'd found anything. Perhaps the discovery about the burial plot was the new evidence, and the police hoped by asking for DNA that they'd pressure him, coerce him into making a confession. A nice fear tactic, but it wasn't going to work. "Sure, I'd be happy to."

The detective was half right. The swab didn't hurt physically, yet the thought of an officer introducing a foreign swab into his mouth disgusted him. Oh sure, the police claimed the procedure was sterile.

Before leaving, the detective warned the Knight that he might need to call him in again as the case progressed. As it progressed...so the Riversdale PD really wasn't going to let this be. The Knight shuddered. He'd worn gloves, but what if the police had found a hair. He snorted. How lousy would that be? Convicted for something as small as that.

As the Knight entered the parking lot and staggered to his car, thoughts of digging up the murder weapon came to mind. Still, then he'd have to devise a plan to relocate it elsewhere. And he wasn't sure he had that much time. First things first. He needed a plan to reveal Mark for who he was and an exit strategy for rescuing Beth and leaving town with her.

And sufficient ammo in case he encountered resistance along the way.

39

That evening, Beth drove to Mark's house. While lasagna cooked in the oven, she reclined on the couch and stared into space, as if in a catatonic trance. The world seemed silent.

Mark exited the kitchen, a dish towel slung over his shoulder. "Something bothering you?"

"Where should I begin?"

Mark sat next to her and put his arm around her. "What's wrong?"

"Budget cuts. My school has to let ten teachers go mid-year, based on seniority, which is fair, but that doesn't exactly help me. I'll know more soon." She rubbed her forehead. "And then my landlord called and reminded me I signed a short-term lease when I moved in, so it's about time to sign again. All I've been thinking about is the layoffs, and I totally forgot. I'm not sure if I should sign another lease. I trust God will provide, but maybe I should look around for another place."

He shook his head and pulled her into a tighter embrace. She leaned her head against his chest. "Beth, I don't think you'll find a better deal, at least not any place where I'd feel comfortable having you stay."

Despite past tragedy, she and Mark had gotten off to a great start. They'd spent two weeks and three wonderful days together. She pulled away from him and rested her hands on her knees. "I do have a bit of money saved up. Maybe I'll sign the lease for another year."

Mark's eyes widened. He played with his shirt collar. "An entire year?"

"You don't think that's a good idea?"

Mark sent her the same look as a middle school student who'd just received a detention. "You should do what you want, but I'd suggest telling your landlord about your situation and see if he'd let you lease on a month-to-month basis."

"My situation? I really wish I knew what that was." She prayed for wisdom then remembered how God brought her and Mark together. Providing a job should be easy compared to that. Besides, this was the God of the universe she was talking to. Nothing was beyond His reach.

40

The Knight needed to lie low, but at the same time, he hoped to uncover more information on Mark, something he could use to prove to Beth that Mark was no good for her.

He'd been monitoring Beth's classroom by webcam. The school district had to make budget cuts, and Beth's position was going to be eliminated. Fools. The Knight had seen her in action and witnessed the compassion she showed toward children. If anything, the district should give Beth a raise. Maybe the Knight ought to leave a surprise for the district office. Teach them not to hurt Beth.

The Knight rubbed his eyes. He refused to become distracted from the problem at hand. Mark Graham. He'd been with Beth when she was attacked and failed to protect her. Now if only the Knight could help her to see this.

On the webcam videos, Beth mentioned to police and other faculty that she'd spent Thanksgiving with her family and Mark. Things were progressing between the two of them. The Knight's breathing became erratic. Hands on his thighs, he closed his eyes and tried not to hyperventilate. Upset about losing her job, Beth might feel further driven into Mark's arms. The Knight gritted his teeth. He very well might have to hasten his plans.

While he lay low, Mark was out there with Beth.

And every day they were together meant another hour she was in danger. He located his notes on Mark's schedule. Each day at 2:00 PM, the housekeeper walked the man's mangy mutt down the street and back and never locked the door. If he could get to Mark's house at that time, and slip inside, maybe he could find something useful, some sort of leverage.

Examining his gun, he loaded the magazine to capacity then shoved it back into the weapon, locking it in place. If Mark or the housekeeper happened to discover him entering the house, he needed to be prepared.

41

Beth slid out of her car and joined Mark outside Fishy Business as he sanded the deck of the *Orange Roughy*. She stared at the ground and kicked at the dirt with her shoes for a few seconds then looked up. Mark had been proud of her when she'd had two jobs. Perhaps his opinion of her might change when he heard her news. "It's official. I'm being let go next month. Didn't even get the chance to start preparing students for the annual spring play. In fact, the play might even get cut." She'd experienced her share of problems in a short lifetime. Why this and why now?

Mark stopped working and looked up at her. "I'm sorry."

If she didn't know better, she'd think he wanted to say more but restrained himself. Her mind raced. Perhaps he wanted to discuss their relationship, maybe even end things but then felt pity because she'd lost her job. She'd whined a lot about her problems lately. Maybe she'd gotten on Mark's last nerve. Probably not the time to mention the notes from the Knight had started again. Considering the notes were probably from someone at the school, Beth shouldn't be receiving them much longer anyway. Once Beth left her job, hopefully, the Knight would move on to annoying someone else.

Besides discussing things with Mark, Beth hesitated to hand over the latest note to the principal.

Looking for a new job, she'd need him for a reference, which meant staying on his good side. The man had expended enough time and manpower as it was to have someone escort her out to car throughout the year. That wouldn't have influenced the district's decision to cut her position, would it? And if she did tell him about her most recent note, all he'd do is reassign a guard to escort her each day. From now on, Beth would simply synchronize her schedule with the math teacher across the hall and walk outside with her.

Beth stuffed her hands in her jean pockets—the same pair she'd worn when first meeting Mark in front of Fishy Business. That's when their relationship had its first spark. And perhaps now it'd come full circle, about to die out. "I guess the good news is my landlord will let me rent on a month-to-month basis. Thanks for suggesting that."

"That's good." Mark furrowed his eyebrows. "Have you looked around to see if the other districts are hiring?"

"A little. I didn't see anything right now. It's hard because it's the middle of the school year. I don't think most districts post their jobs for the next year just yet. But I guess maybe I could sub."

Mark's bicep flexed as he held up his sanding tool then looked at her. "That's a good idea." He'd been going to the gym more lately. Working on a community college campus, who knew how many women he came in contact with. Regardless, he was bound to turn some heads with his rugged good looks. Frazzled and worried about her job, Beth hadn't taken good care of herself lately. Fingering split ends, she realized her hair desperately needed a trim.

"Yeah, but I heard some of the other teachers say it

doesn't pay that well. I'm also concerned that so many other teachers will be looking for positions."

"God's still in control, right?"

She bit back a grin. "Last time I checked. I suppose you're right."

Mark motioned to her. "Come help me." An invitation to join him. Far better than a rejection.

Beth walked up on the boat, grabbed a sanding tool, and helped him finish the deck. God was in control, yet He decided to take Chris away and now her job. What next?

42

The Knight prepared for his big day. He studied his notes, going over them until he could recite them from memory.

At 1:45 PM, he drove one block from Mark's home and walked down the man's street, hiding in a bush across from the house.

At 2:02 PM, as soon as the housekeeper and the dog were out of range, the Knight slipped inside the house. At most, he had four minutes to get in and out. After scanning two bedrooms, he decided the most lived-in must be Mark's. The Knight reflected on where he'd keep his own personal belongings and opened the man's closet door. A box sat atop a shelf, and he opened it. A notebook lay inside, along with some photos. He snatched a photo and the notebook and glanced at his watch. Two minutes—he'd better go. After he replaced the box, he closed the closet door and went out the back. The Knight waited by the gate in the backyard until the housekeeper and the dog walked near the front door. The front door slammed, and he let himself into the front yard, closing the gate behind him. Then he crossed through the neighbor's yard and walked around the block to his car, not stopping until he got there.

He got into the driver's seat and stared at the photo. Mark stood next to another man. Both appeared younger and were dressed in fatigues. The other looked a bit like Beth. He set the photo aside, opened the notebook, and began reading.

Pretty mundane everyday stuff. Life in the Corps. Blah, blah, and then...Whoa. Yeah, good thing he was protecting Beth from Mark.

A curse escaped his lips. So he wasn't the only one with dark secrets. The Knight skipped his fingers along the edge of the notebook. Here was his golden ticket. With it, he could blackmail Mark and use it to win over Beth. The Knight hoped Beth would join him willingly. Murder was messy. He wasn't sure he was up to cleaning up after another one.

43

Pulling the curtains to one side, Mark gazed out his living room window, waiting for Beth to arrive. A strange green car parked outside across the street attracted his attention. He didn't remember seeing it before. Perhaps he should ask around to see if it belonged to one of the neighbors.

He sighed. Still no sign of Beth.

Two weeks had passed since she'd lost her job. He hoped a relaxing dinner might cheer her up. It was worth a try.

A minute later, she pulled into his driveway, and he walked outside to meet her.

"Hi." Mark opened the door, greeted Beth with a kiss, then led her inside. At the same time, an engine started, and the green car pulled away from the curb. He shifted his gaze to Beth. "I hope you brought your appetite."

Beth's lips formed a faint smile.

He'd hoped by now she'd find another job. If only he had more for her to do at Fishy Business, he'd hire her back in a heartbeat. Maybe if he kept his ears open, something might open up at the community college, and he could help her find a position there.

They walked through his house then out to his yard. Beth sat at a picnic table and scratched Sparky's head while Mark grilled dinner.

Mark turned the meat on the grill. "Want to go to

the movies this Saturday?"

"Huh? Oh, sure. But I probably should walk around the mall first and pick up some applications."

No matter what he said, he couldn't take her mind off the problem at hand. Or could he?

After finishing their meals, they sat outside and watched the evening sunset while Sparky romped around.

His lips brushed her cheek, but she remained unfazed.

Sparky scampered over and brought Beth a tennis ball. For a moment, she appeared to smile, but then she threw the ball and stared into the distance.

The dog returned and dropped the ball in front of them then lay on the ground, kicking his back legs behind him.

Perhaps her sadness came from more than the layoffs. Mark rested a hand on Beth's shoulder. "Still thinking about the job situation?"

Beth nodded. "I've saved up some money over the past few months, which is good."

"But...?"

"But I'm concerned how long I'll be out of work." She remained quiet for a moment, bit her lip, then sent him a look that told him he wasn't going to like what she had to say. "I found a teaching job in Columbus."

C-bus. Not exactly next door. His shoulders tensed.

"I like it here, and I want to stay. But eventually my savings will run out. I don't want to go, but I..." She choked back a sob.

He grabbed her hand. "Let me help you. I could sell the boat."

Beth shook her head. "I can't take your money,

and you should keep your boat." She wiped her tear-soaked eyes.

He hung his head. He'd fallen in love with her. If he didn't move fast, he might lose her forever. A chance he wasn't willing to take.

There was so much he wanted to tell her, but the timing was off. Or maybe it wasn't. How could he be sure?

❧

Mark drove over to Bill's place. Perhaps his friend could provide some insight into the current situation.

He knocked on the door, and Bill answered. "Come on in."

Stepping inside, Mark peeked around the living room. "Tim here?"

Bill slumped into his weathered black leather couch. "Nope. What's up?"

Not sure where to begin, he sat next to his friend and folded his hands. "Beth is considering taking a teaching position in Columbus. Obviously, I don't want her to leave so..." He rubbed a callous on his left hand.

Bill snatched the remote from his coffee table and turned off the Syfy Channel. "Ah...that does change things. So have you told her anything yet?"

"No, I—"

"Well, not the one thing, of course. But, the other...you haven't said anything about"—Bill cleared his throat—"you-know-what?"

"I don't know how. I was praying that—"

"When you first ran into her, I totally understood your reasons for not saying anything, for waiting, but now… How can you not tell her?"

Easy for his friend to say. He wasn't the one risking a relationship with the woman he loved. Still, if their relationship was to go further, he'd have to be honest, even if it hurt.

Bill tapped his fingers on the remote. "What happens if she finds out from someone else?"

"What do you mean?"

His friend shrugged. "I think she'd prefer to hear things from you."

Not many people knew. Those who did weren't about to say anything. Then again, secrets seem to have a way of haunting people, coming out at the wrong time. "You're right, absolutely right. I'll tell her. Thanks."

"Hey, anytime."

He stood, and Bill patted him on the back. "She loves you, and you'll work through this. I'm not saying it'll be easy. Maybe you'll need to talk to someone. But you both have a strong faith in God, and I'm sure that'll get you through this."

Waving good-bye, Mark headed home. Upon entering his bedroom, he walked to his closet and stared at the box on the top shelf. Maybe it was time to deal with the past. Writing had helped him before. Maybe it would again.

Sparky sighed, and Mark scratched the dog's head. "Time for bed, little man?" Mark could journal about things later. For now, he needed a good night's sleep and some prayer.

He climbed into bed, Sparky by his side on the floor. *God, give me the words to say to Beth. And please don't let her run away from me.*

44

Still invigorated from his talk with Bill the day before, Mark called Beth and made evening plans. He'd take her to dinner and a movie then get coffee and stop by the lighthouse. She seemed to like the place. Maybe that'd be the best location to break the news to her.

He picked her up around six thirty. They went to the Chinese buffet at the mall.

Beth finished a bite of her sesame chicken. "You can relax and not worry about Antonio riding into town on a white horse and trying to woo me away."

Mark folded his arms. "Oh, really. Why's that?"

"Apparently, he eloped with his high school sweetheart and moved to Oregon."

"Interesting." Maybe Antonio felt motivated by fear of losing the woman he loved. As long as that woman wasn't Beth, good for him.

After dinner, the two of them headed toward Riversdale Cinemas. Mark remembered he needed to stop by Fishy Business and make sure the back door was locked. It'd take him a moment, and they'd be on their way to the movies. He might even have time to grab a soda. His mouth remained on fire from the Kung Pao he'd eaten.

"Whose cars are those?" Beth pointed to a green vehicle with someone inside, parked at the far end of the lot next to two other cars, one yellow, one red.

"Probably from Fan Fare next door. They don't have much parking, so some of their patrons park here. As long as they're not causing problems, I don't care." Another reason to check the lock. He and Beth ambled to the door, and he checked the knob—just as it should be. Using his key, he let them inside then walked to the cooler and retrieved a soft drink. "Do you want something to drink?"

Beth nodded then chuckled.

"Care to tell me what's so funny?"

"Just thinking about the day we ran into each other. About how I had car trouble, and you came out and offered me a soda."

A knock sounded, and Mark shifted his gaze toward a man looking at him through the windowpane at the top of the door. "Randy?"

"I thought he didn't work here anymore," Beth said. "And why's he wearing…gloves?"

Mark set down his drink and opened the door. "What are you doing here so late?"

Eyebrows arched, the man's gaze pierced Mark. "I could ask you the same question."

"Huh? Look, I don't think we need anything refilled right now, but thanks."

"I'm not here to refill things. Came here to find out more. And imagine my good fortune running into the two of you." Randy removed a notebook from behind his back and waved it in front of Mark. "Look familiar?" His gaze moved to Beth.

Blue, spiral, three ring, and distinctive drawings on the outside. "Hey, that's mine. Where'd you get that?" Mark reached for the item, but Randy pulled it away.

Randy tucked the notebook under his arm. "Let's

just say, I came into possession of it."

Mark took a step forward, towering over Randy. "You mean you stole it."

"Making accusations, Mark? Not nice. Especially when I could make a few of my own. This diary of yours, thought-provoking material. I'm sure Beth might be interested in the contents."

No way. He reached for the diary, but Randy dropped the notebook and brandished a gun.

Mark's senses jumped to full attention. The man waved the weapon in front of them and nodded toward Beth. "You can tell her the truth, or I can. What'll it be?"

Mark put his hands up and moved closer to Beth, attempting to shield her. An emotional interplay. Smart move on the other guy's part. Now if only he could keep his head straight and his mind focused.

Beth grabbed his shoulder. "Tell me what?"

Not now. The moment Mark had dreaded the past eleven years, and at a time when he needed more than anything to stay focused on the gun. "Beth, I wanted to tell you. But I didn't know how." He kept a gun in the work desk. The problem would be getting to it without being noticed.

"What do you mean?" Beth asked. "I thought you'd told me everything about your condition."

Randy stepped toward Beth. "When your brother died…" He turned his head at an awkward angle. A wild and bizarre grin formed on his face—the sides of his mouth lifted at awkward and unnatural angles. "Know how it happened?"

Beth glanced between Mark and Randy. "An ambush."

Randy leaned against the side of the desk and

chuckled.

Here it came. The gory details were headed toward Beth faster than a cruise missile. And Mark couldn't stop it. But if he could stop Randy from hurting them…Mark shifted his gaze to the middle desk drawer, near where the man stood.

"Right. An ambush. I'm guessing Mark neglected to mention the presence of friendly fire." Randy shook his head. "Can't imagine why."

"Friendly fire? No. No, I don't believe it." She glared at Randy then faced Mark. "Tell him it isn't true."

"Beth, I wish I could." He was going to have to wrestle for the weapon. There was no other choice. He might get shot, but at least he could save Beth.

"You shot him?" She covered her mouth with her hand.

"Someone in our unit did. I was in charge. I didn't see the ambush coming. Chris went down, and I tried to save him. I failed him."

"After you shot him?" Randy's smile turned to a grotesque frown. "You said you were guilty. You wrote about it."

Emotions overrode his focus on the weapon, and Mark touched her arm. "I *feel* guilty. It wasn't my gun that killed him, but I was still in charge. Under my command, Chris was killed as a result of friendly fire."

Beth sobbed. "No, this can't be happening." She stepped away from Mark. "I can't believe you didn't tell me. So he wasn't killed by the enemy. He was killed by his friends." She narrowed her gaze. "Was it Bill? Tim? What about Kent? What else have you been keeping from me?"

"Beth, I'll never tell you. The military dealt with it.

In combat—"

"First you neglect to tell me about the post-traumatic stress disorder and the fact that you can walk, and now this. How can ever I trust you?" She leaned nearer to him. "How can I ever get close to you?"

Randy holstered his gun, grabbed Beth's hand, and dragged her away. "C'mon, Beth. You deserve a real man, a whole man, someone better."

Mark reached for Beth, but his legs buckled beneath him. He slumped to the ground and put his hand to his head, but the pounding wouldn't stop. His feet failed to cooperate. He couldn't move. No, not again. Not another episode, now of all times. He tried to tell himself that it was all in his head—work himself out of the episode, but his legs refused to cooperate.

Words came from Beth's mouth, but Mark's mind kept spinning. He tried to grip the wall to help him stand. He fought a losing battle, relying only on his upper body strength.

"Mark, please." Beth reached toward him.

Randy dragged Beth to the door. They'd gotten that far.

Beth kicked and screamed. "Mark, don't listen to him. It's in your mind. Your legs are fine. You can walk!" Again she screamed. "Get up, Mark. Help me. I forgive you."

45

She was feistier than he imagined. The Knight would give Beth that. Juanita had not struggled as much when he'd kidnapped her from her new boyfriend's apartment. With Mark slumped on the floor inside the building, Beth should accept her fate as well.

If only she had the opportunity to get to know him better, get to know the real him, then she'd feel differently. She was smart. He'd handpicked her, so he ought to know—so smart that she had to eventually see things from his perspective. And if not…if not, then he'd have to opt for Plan B. He glanced at the Sig Sauer on his holster belt. Still there, still loaded, ready to be used if necessary. Outside the building, the Knight reached into his pocket to remove his key fob. He held Beth against him, one arm wrapped around her.

At the same time, Beth kicked against the side of the building, apparently in an attempt to break free. He dropped his keys. "Oh no, you don't." He grabbed her left arm, leaned over into her ear, and whispered. "The rules to this game are very important, Beth." Using his right hand, he grabbed his Sig and pressed against the small of her back. "Those who don't play by them"— he tightened his grip on her—"get hurt. I help you, and in return, you accept my help. And if you can't accept my help, then I'll protect you in other ways, whatever the cost. But at least Mark won't be able to hurt you anymore." With the gun focused on her, he reached down and grabbed his keys with his free hand and unlocked his car.

"God, please help me," she said.

Beth believed in a deity? So much for smart. "Go ahead and pray to your Creator. It won't make a difference." He'd prayed when his stepdad beat him, and nothing happened.

Beth screamed and struggled some more. "Mark! Help!"

The Knight dragged her next to the passenger side of his car and opened the door. "You don't need him, Beth. You've got me. I'm your knight. I'll keep you safe. I'm here to protect you. I won't let him harm you anymore. I know you didn't like it when he called you 'little,' but I think there's nothing wrong with your height. And any guy who'd allow your brother to get shot by his own troops and not tell you isn't the one for you."

He grinned. He'd rescued Beth, and he'd done it all without those stupid pills the doctor had prescribed. His heart raced. He sucked in a deep breath, more alive than ever before.

46

Though Beth and Randy stumbled outside, Beth's words lingered and penetrated Mark. It *was* in his mind. And she'd forgiven him. A weight dropped from his body. *Dear God, help me.* Warmth flooded his feet and his legs. A miracle. *Thank you, God.*

He struggled twice to gain his balance then stood up. Staring at the notebook Randy had left behind, guilt riddled him, and he began to stumble again. Mark closed his eyes and replayed Beth's words. His mind might be weak, but his legs were able. He opened his eyes, ran to the desk, grabbed the gun from the desk drawer, and dashed outside.

Randy was gone—and Beth with him.

He dialed 9-1-1 and gave the operator the details. What now? Sit back and wait for the cops to find Randy and Beth? Not good enough. One thing was certain. Randy would take Beth back to his place, wherever that was.

Mark sprinted inside and shook the mouse to wake up the computer. Logging on, he soon accessed scans of receipts from the vending company that contained Randy's signature—Randy Smith. Mark snorted. Smith? Like that was the man's real last name.

Mark opened an Internet browser. An hourglass icon lingered on the screen. "Ugh. Come on." He slammed his hand on the desk. The screen remained frozen for a moment but then loaded, one useless graphic at a time. Using the mouse, he moved his cursor to a search bar and began to type. His fingers moved faster than the letters appeared on screen. He clicked on the search button. Nothing. He clicked to stop loading the browser. The page stopped loading just as the search results began to appear on the screen. "Noooo!" He shoved the keyboard away then rubbed his forehead. "Get a hold on yourself, Corporal." He reloaded the page then removed his fingers from the keyboard. As the hourglass again turned on the screen, he fought the urge to throw the computer against the wall. Instead he turned away, clenched and unclenched his fists, and then swung back to the screen. His breath came out in a swoosh. "Randy Smith, Riversdale, 1312 Kumquat Court." Bingo. He removed a notepad from the desk drawer and jotted down the address.

Keys in his pocket, Mark scrambled toward his van and punched the address in the GPS. With a bit of cloud cover, the GPS unit took a few minutes to acquire a strong signal. More precious time wasted.

He used his Bluetooth to call Bill. "You were right, I'm afraid. Someone else told her my secret first."

"What do you mean?"

He quickly explained to his friend what had ensued.

"Hold on." Bill spoke in the background. "OK, Tim's dialing 9-1-1 and asking them to send some officers to that address you gave me."

"Don't hang up. I need you to keep talking with me. Do what my therapist said. Stay on the line and remind me that it's all in my head. Can you do that?"

"You got it."

Mark accelerated the vehicle as the light turned

green. Time was of the essence. Extra minutes could cost Beth her life. *Dear God, please protect her. I don't know how, but please make time stand still.* Maybe he could reach her before the police could.

ॐॐ

Beth stared out the car window. Randy had locked the doors using the master control. His gun sat on the console between them.

He caught her eyeing it then moved it to the driver's side door storage bin. "Tsk, tsk. And don't think about trying the doors. I have child safety locks. It's for your own good…to help keep you safe."

No way out, at least not at the moment.

He glanced at her. "It's OK now, Beth. You don't have to see him anymore."

"You don't understand. I forgive him for what he did."

Randy grunted. "Please. My stepfather beat me. Mark caused your brother's death. You can't forgive stuff like that."

"But God forgives us."

"I hate to tell you, but God doesn't exist." Anger inflected in his voice.

Oh yes, He does. Not like she could explain that to this lunatic.

Randy pulled onto another street, this one less populated than the last. "Now, I just need to go home and get a few things before we head to my other apartment. I have more of those books with funny signs. I know how much you liked the one I let you borrow. We also need to stop by the cemetery to say good-bye to a friend, and then we can head out of town. Soon, we can put this all behind us."

Cemetery? Chills spread over her. *God, give me peace.* A sense of calm washed over her. No matter what happened, live or die, she had God.

A car in front of them blew exhaust in their direction. Beth sneezed.

"You have to watch out for germs. It's very important." Randy grabbed a box of hand wipes from the side compartment and handed them to her. "Clean your hands, then toss the offending wipe outside."

Doing as he instructed, she wiped down her hands and forearms thoroughly.

Randy let the window down. "No funny business. It's my job to protect you."

She tossed the wipe outside, hoping she'd sloughed off some skin cells during her cleaning. Maybe someone might find her DNA.

The car came to a stop. Randy put her window back up. She studied her captor. This man feared germs. Maybe she could use this to her advantage. Sure he had a gun, but perhaps she could wield a different weapon.

47

The Knight drove for another block but cringed as Beth let out another sneeze. He wrestled with a thought. Should he kill her to protect her from her own germs? Nah, he'd just need to teach her how to avoid them in the future. And be sure to pop a few pills once they got back to his house.

Beth sneezed again. "I think I'm coming down with something. Do you think maybe we could stop by the drugstore on Fourth Street?"

"Now? We don't have time. Besides, then we have to change our route. I hadn't planned on going that direction."

"But, it will be fun. The drugstore has these silly cards there I want to show you. And then we can pick up some allergy medication and something to drink because I'm a little thirsty. And if we're stopping by the cemetery, maybe we should get some flowers."

Not a bad idea. Juanita might appreciate the gesture. "But what about Mark?"

"What about him? You showed him who was boss. I don't think he's going to give us any trouble."

Could this be for real? Had Beth changed her tune this easily? "So you're really starting to see things from my perspective." He bit his lip. "I don't know what to say."

"Like you said, I'm a smart girl." Beth coughed a few times and grabbed several wipes for her hands and then washed down the surrounding seat and console area. "Yeah, we probably should get more of these too. I might be coming down with something, and I wouldn't want to spread germs all over your nice car." Again she coughed. "I'm just so sorry. Would you prefer I sit in the back?"

The Knight gritted his teeth. "No!"

So Beth was smart but sick. Despite all his planning and calculating, something he hadn't counted on. She probably got germs from being around Mark and his mangy mutt.

He didn't want to stop. They'd only waste time. And what if Mark did try to find them? Then what? Still, Beth didn't feel well, and if he didn't try to help her, what kind of knight would he be? Plus, he could refill his prescription while he was there. At the rate germs were leaving Beth's body, he might need to double up on his dose just to get through this evening.

48

Mark slammed his fist on the steering wheel. Red flashing lights and a train signal teased him. His vehicle sat behind several others, awaiting a train he doubted would show up. All the while, Randy had Beth.

Mark stepped out of his van to stretch his legs. It wasn't like he was going anywhere anyway. Bill stayed on the phone with him and occasionally reminded him that his physical maladies were psychosomatic.

Once out of the vehicle, Mark took a few steps forward and to the left of his van. *God, can it be?* A green car like the one parked by Fishy Business...like the one that had been parked in front of his house. Somehow he'd overlooked the similarities.

Mark slipped back into the van. A train of cars sat wedged between his and Randy's. "Bill, you still there?"

"I'm here."

"You're not going to believe this. I'm stopped at the train crossing by the abandoned paper mill near Citrus Avenue. A bunch of cars are in front of me. At the front of the line is Randy. I'm sure of it."

"Hold on." Bill mumbled something. "OK, Tim's dialing 9-1-1 again. We'll have someone meet you there. Maybe you should wait until the cops arrive. Don't try to be heroic."

Bill didn't mean it in a bad way, but that word

bothered him. He was no hero. He hadn't saved Chris's life. And maybe he'd fail to save Beth's, too.

The whistle of an approaching train sounded. He sized up the oncoming locomotive. He could risk it and hope it'd buy him time until the cops arrived. *God, please give me wisdom.*

"Hey, Mark," Bill said, "Tim says the evening trains aren't that long."

Mark shook his head. Not the best place for a rescue. His mind flashed to the night Chris died. Beth's own brother had been killed by friendly fire. What if an innocent bystander, not to mention Beth, was injured, maybe even killed in the attempt to save her?

So many what ifs. Including what if Randy made off with Beth before the police or Mark could apprehend him. Mark shuddered. This might be the only chance for him to save the woman he loved. He'd try to disarm Randy without using a weapon if possible, but even if not, Mark still needed to take the chance. He flung open the van door and jogged several vehicles closer. Two cars remained between him and a madman.

He inched his way closer and stooped to pick up a rock. With great force, he threw it at the window of the car then crouched behind the vehicle.

Randy opened the driver's side door and leaned toward the passenger's side. "Beth, stay put," he yelled.

Mark stood and moved toward Randy, gun at the ready.

The man stepped out of the car and began to turn around.

Mark slipped his gun in his waistband and jumped the man from behind. "Beth, duck!" He tackled

Randy to the ground, preferring to subdue the man rather than shoot him, if possible.

The man moved his gun toward Mark.

Mark pushed the gun out of the way.

Randy struggled to move the firearm closer again.

Mark wrapped his hands around the gun, redirected it away from traffic, then pulled the trigger, firing a shot.

Randy tensed, and Mark slid the weapon across the pavement. The man scrambled toward it.

Mark pointed his gun at Randy. "Let it go."

"Or what?" Randy reached for his weapon.

Time to stop the threat at hand. Mark aimed and fired.

Randy fell, and again, reached for his gun. He began to lift the weapon, swinging it toward Mark.

Mark fired again. The slug slammed into Randy's chest. Mark dashed toward Randy and kicked the gun away. With the man subdued, Mark shifted his gaze toward the car.

Beth stood from a crouched position outside the vehicle and moved toward him.

"Are you OK?" Mark asked.

Beth nodded.

Mark leaned over to check Randy's pulse. Faint but present. Mark's head pounded. He visually measured Randy's blood loss.

"Should we call 9-1-1?" Beth asked.

"Already on their way. Tim called them for me. And I'm sure some of the drivers in the others cars have phoned this in by now." Sure help was coming, but from the looks of Randy's wounds, it'd be too late. Another person dead on Mark's watch. His hand shook as he tucked his gun in his waistband.

Beth grabbed his hand and rubbed it. "You had to do it. It was self-defense. If you didn't shoot him, he would have shot us."

"Is everyone OK? What's going on here?" A stout older gentleman with squinty eyes glared at Mark.

Beth pointed at Randy. "That man has been sending me strange notes, and he kidnapped me." She touched Mark's shoulder. "But my boyfriend saved me."

Mark hung his head. He was no hero. *Thank you, God. You're the one who saved us all. In more ways than one.* He made eye contact with the elderly man. "The police should be here any minute."

"I'll give my statement to the authorities. Saw the whole thing." The man held out his hand to Beth. "I'm Pete Brown, retired police officer, ma'am. If what you're saying is true, young lady, then that's quite a hero you've got here." He thumbed toward Mark. "You better keep him around."

Beth's eyes twinkled. "That's what I'd like to do."

Mark wanted that as well, but even more than that, he wanted to get away from this scene and have a chance to talk to Beth, to discuss what happened.

The last of the train roared along the tracks.

"I'd move that vehicle," Pete offered, "but it'd contaminate a crime scene. I'll ask the other drivers to pull off to the side of the road and wait for the police to arrive." Pete walked up to the car behind his to explain the situation to the driver then directed where to park. Other cars followed suit.

Mark handed Beth his keys. "Can you move the van, please?"

"Sure." She walked off and parked the vehicle near the side of the road.

The paramedics arrived but waited off to the side, four police officers close behind. So much for discussing things with Beth.

Two of the officers worked to secure the scene. The first officer approached Mark. "I'll need your weapon."

Mark handed over the gun.

The second officer collected Randy's weapon.

The first officer separated Mark and Beth. "Please go stand by the other police vehicle, ma'am. As for you, sir, I'm going to need you to put your hands behind your back and lean up against the vehicle."

Mark did as told, and the officer patted him down, presumably ensuring he didn't have another weapon. A moment later, the cold touch of metal handcuffs grazed Mark's wrists. He'd done nothing wrong, and yet, once the officer cuffed Mark, he stowed him in the back of a police cruiser. "I need you to wait in here while we sort things out."

Two other cops motioned for paramedics to enter the scene. They rushed in, examined Randy, loaded him onto a stretcher, and covered him with a white sheet. Not a bad idea considering the crowd that was forming. The two other cops appeared to be conversing with paramedics. No sirens blared as the ambulance left without Randy's body, presumably for a medical examiner to contend with; the eerie absence of the siren jolted Mark back to the reality of what happened. He hadn't been involved in a firefight in years. And yet, he didn't suffer from an episode. One thing kept him going. The hope that Beth had truly forgiven him.

Meanwhile, the other officers walked around from car to car and appeared to be taking statements from the passengers.

The officer who had spoken to Mark opened the back of the adjacent police cruiser and escorted Beth inside. Must have been standard procedure, and yet, Mark clenched his jaw. Beth had been through enough in her life. She didn't deserve this.

The other officer spoke to Beth for quite some time, at least while the three other officers released the bystanders from the scene and made their way back to their vehicles.

What would happen to him? He'd shot Randy for no other reason than to protect Beth and in self-defense. Surely, he wouldn't be charged with excessive force. *Lord, you know I acted in self-defense and to protect Beth. Please help the police to straighten things out.*

The other officer released Beth then returned to his vehicle. Beth appeared to make a phone call. Several minutes later, Marisa arrived and hugged Beth.

Mark caught a glimpse of an unreadable look from Beth as she ducked into Marisa's car. Was Beth angry with him? She'd said she'd forgiven him, but maybe only because of the heat of the moment. Perhaps she'd changed her mind. The officer cleared his throat before asking Mark another question, returning him to the reality of the present.

After what seemed like an eternity of interrogation, the officer stared down at Mark. "Let's get these cuffs off of you. You're free to go. The evidence shows you acted in self-defense as well as in defense of your girlfriend."

As he left the crime scene, Mark realized there was only one place he wanted to be. And yet, Beth needed her rest. He'd visit her tomorrow. He rubbed a knot in his right shoulder. It wouldn't hurt him to get some shut-eye, too.

As he got into his van, he realized how close he'd come to losing Beth. Losing Chris was one thing. Losing Beth, too, another. Mark's body shook, and he tried to make sense of his feelings.

49

The early morning sun glared through the windshield as Mark parked his van in front of Beth's apartment.

Mark shifted the weight of a cardboard coffee carrier into his left hand while he knocked on the door.

Beth opened the door; eyes red and watery. A fresh tear streamed down her face. "I spoke to the police about what happened and mentioned how Randy told me about another woman in a cemetery. I'm guessing I'm not the first person he'd harassed. They gave me the name of a victim's advocate. After that, I called Marisa, and she drove me home." She rushed toward him and grasped his forearms. "Are you okay?"

Mark freed himself from Beth's hold, ambled to the coffee table, and set down the cardboard carrier. "I'm fine." He tipped Beth's chin. "The real question is, are *you* okay?"

She nodded.

"Brought some coffee. Hazelnut for me and minty mocha for you." She reached for her coffee and took a sip. "Thanks."

He stared at her. "You meant what you said last night?"

She returned her coffee to the carrier. "That I forgive you? Yeah. I know you loved Chris like a brother. You'd never hurt him intentionally." She took a deep breath. "I won't ask you who did shoot him. I have to forgive and let go. God's forgiven me. What right do I have to hold a grudge?"

"We can go to counseling, talk to someone about it. I'm willing to do whatever it takes to work through this. If you're OK with that."

Moving closer, she wrapped her arms around him in a tight embrace.

As a barrage of tears streamed down her already moist face, Mark moved back, then put one hand behind Beth's head and leaned over to kiss her. Though the elderly bystander near the railroad crossing had called Mark a hero when he'd rescued Beth, Mark wasn't sure he fit the bill. And yet, hero or not, he wanted to hold her forever and not let go. Drawing her head against his chest, he stroked her hair and held her close.

Taking a glance at the nighttime sky, he released his breath and relaxed his shoulders a little. Beth knew his secret and still forgave him.

Years of heavy guilt and pain fell from his chest. The God of all comfort had not forgotten him.

❧❦

Around late afternoon, Beth met Mark in front of her apartment. She locked her front door then scanned the parking lot.

Mark stood face-to-face with her and grabbed her shoulders. "It's over now, Beth. Randy's dead. You're safe."

She nodded and leaned forward. Their lips interlocked. Moving to Columbus would kill her. But there was no other way.

As they walked to Mark's van, he put his arm around her. "You ready for some fun?"

She wasn't, but neither was she going to put a damper on their picnic, perhaps their last one together. Unseasonably warm winter weather provided an excellent backdrop for their outdoor plans.

When they arrived at the store, Mark had barely put the vehicle in park before Bill and Tim, clad in grilling aprons, greeted them.

The four friends enjoyed lunch at the picnic table on the patio outside the store and watched boats arrive in the nearby marina. Owners strung lights on the exterior of their vessels.

Beth fanned herself with a plate. Once they'd all finished eating, she threw her plate in the trash and winked at Tim. "My compliments to the chef."

Bill removed a pack of gum from his pocket, took out a piece, and offered one to his brother. "Hey, I want to try out some of the new bait we received yesterday."

Tim slowly stuck the gum in his mouth and stared at Mark.

Mark waved his hands dismissively. "Go on. Take the boat without me. I trust you two."

"Why don't you come with us?" Tim asked.

"No, thanks."

Tim scratched his head. "So why are you concerned about this particular shipment of bait?"

Bill touched Tim's shoulder. "I'd like to go fishing with my little brother. Is that OK?"

"OK." Tim looked at Mark and Beth. "Guess we'll see you two later."

Perhaps she should have spoken up, but it wasn't her boat. It might have been fun to go out on the pontoon to catch a better glimpse of the lights in harbor. Plus, they were sure to have good seats for the marina winter fireworks and lights display. Maybe the guys would be back in time for the fireworks.

"We'll be back in about two hours," Bill said. He and Tim waved and headed out the back of the store.

Mark walked over to her. "Can you help me with something?"

"Sure." Beth followed him inside the store.

"I left some bait containers by the cash register. Would you mind getting them for me?"

So he'd rather sort bait than go out on the boat. At least they'd get to spend time together. If she moved to Columbus, Beth wouldn't be seeing much of him. She'd better enjoy her time with him while she could.

Beth ambled to the register and grabbed six containers nearby. As she picked them up, she noticed something inside the top container. She walked to the back of the store and set the containers on a desk. "Mark, what are these?" She held up a pair of military dog tags.

He didn't answer. Perhaps he hadn't heard her.

"Mark, are these yours? I think you left these in one of the containers." She dangled the tags in front of his face.

Mark stared blankly, sitting at the desk. His business ledger book lay wide open in front of him. "Those aren't my tags. I have mine on me. Check the name."

"Do you think maybe they belong to Tim or Bill?"

Mark turned his back toward Beth. "I'd check the name."

She looked down at the tags then away and then down again. "Wait, I don't get it."

He closed his ledger and looked up at her. "What is it? Is something wrong?"

She studied the tags. "It says Elizabeth Graham on the tags. Mark?"

Mark beamed. "You could say I was feeling confident you'd say yes." He got up from his chair, dropped down on one knee, and pulled out a Tiffany cut diamond ring. He held it out, awaiting her response. "Elizabeth Martindale, will you have a fun summer with me, and not just one summer, but many more?"

She covered her mouth with her hand.

Sweat beaded on Mark's brow.

Beth looked him in the eyes. "Are you serious?"

Mark nodded.

She bent down to him and closed her eyes. Her lips met his and lingered there for a moment.

He pulled back. "I take that as a yes?"

"Yes, yes, of course."

He placed the ring on her finger.

"Mark, it's beautiful."

He took a deep breath and sighed. "It was my grandmother's engagement ring."

Beth fixed her gaze on the ring then shifted it to Mark. "You didn't do this just to get me to stay, did you?"

Mark stuffed his hand in his pockets and stared at the ground. "No, I've had this planned for some time. Originally, I was going to wait until Valentine's Day."

Wooziness threatened to overtake her. She steadied herself.

He smiled and crossed his arms. "I talked to a friend who works at U.C. San Diego. He thinks he can help me get a job there. It pays better, but then I probably wouldn't have time to work at Fishy Business, so I was hoping maybe you could work here, that is, until you find another teaching job."

"Wow, you've really thought this through." Who might she share the good news with first? "I should call my mom."

Mark grinned.

"She already knows?"

He shrugged. "Call me old fashioned, but I called your dad first."

"You asked for permission? Very cool." She studied Mark's face. "I'm assuming he said yes."

A knowing look appeared on his face.

She held out her hand, admiring the twinkling stone. Warmth flooded her. "I don't know when we should get married, but I do know where."

Mark leaned closer.

She turned to face him. "If you're OK with it"— Beth put her hands on his shoulders—"I think we should get married in Beaumont."

"That's not a bad idea."

"Oh, but what about our friends here?" Not everyone might be able to attend a wedding in Ohio.

"We can have a reception here with them later."

"Excellent idea."

A loud boom resounded, and a brilliant light flashed in the distance.

She sat next to him and shifted her gaze to the back door. "I think it's the fireworks."

Mark put his arm around her. "We should probably go outside and watch them, don't you think?"

Beth looked up at him. "I agree."

A loud bang.

Mark stopped still in his tracks.

Beth leaned toward him and gazed at his hand. It wasn't shaking. Still, he might be suffering from a flashback. "Are you OK?"

Mark grinned. "Yeah, yeah, I am."

Beth walked outside with Mark. Sailboats covered with thin strands of small white lights stood docked in the bayside marina.

Mark slipped his arm around her, and she rested in his embrace.

Their reflections glimmered below on the water's surface. Could there be a more perfect evening? Off on the horizon, opposite the harbor, fireworks climbed higher and higher. The magnificent explosions burst into brilliant colors that lit the nighttime sky—a sight as bright as the future that lay ahead of them.

Epilogue

At the wedding reception dinner, Mark sat at the head table, surrounded by family and friends. Pink and purple floral centerpieces decorated the tables. The scents of vanilla and roses pervaded the room.

Mark breathed a sigh of relief—So much had occurred to get him to this moment: sitting beside Mrs. Beth Graham, the new, not to mention the prettiest, English teacher at Riversdale Middle School. The only love notes she'd receive in the future would come from him.

Considering the oppressive humidity of Ohio summers, Mark was thankful Beth consented to an indoor wedding in June.

Tim leaned closer to him. "So the bridesmaid I walked down the aisle with. What's her story?"

Mark shook his head. "Rachel? She's a friend of Beth's from high school. Come to think of it, don't Bill and you fly home tomorrow? If you want to talk to her, better do it now."

Tim scrambled to his feet, moved toward Rachel, and began chatting.

Mark chuckled and glanced at Bill. "Can you believe that?"

Bill shook his head.

After cutting their three-tiered cake adorned with pastel flowers, Mark and Beth rejoined the bridal party at the head table.

Mark turned to talk to his bride, but once again, someone else had started a conversation with her. "I'm beginning to think I might need an appointment to speak with my wife," he glanced at Bill and chuckled. "You haven't touched your cake yet."

"Huh?"

He followed Bill's gaze across the room to a table in front of them. "Wait a minute. I see what's going on here. You've been awful quiet and staring in that direction for a while. I should have known." Mark leaned closer to Bill and whispered, "That girl you've been eyeing. That's Marisa. Beth's neighbor."

Bill's face turned red, and he fidgeted with his collar. "Who said I was asking?"

Mark patted his friend on the back. "Yeah, right."

Guests flooded by the bridal party table to congratulate Mark and Beth. Mark began to sit, but the photographer directed Mark and Beth to stand and pose for several more pictures. After twenty minutes of photos, Mark took a seat and released a sigh. And to think, they'd get to repeat this once they traveled back home to California.

After the guests left the reception hall, he and Beth changed into jeans and t-shirts and helped her family take down decorations.

Her parents were the last to say good-bye. "I couldn't imagine a better son-in-law," Mr. Martindale nodded then grabbed Mark, giving him a bear hug.

"Thanks, sir."

Mr. Martindale assumed the tone and stature of a commanding officer. "That's Dad to you from now on."

"Yes, sir. Uh…Dad."

Once he and Beth finished their good-byes, Mrs.

Martindale grabbed her husband by the arm and walked toward the door. "C'mon, it's time to go."

Mark glanced at the cake.

Beth put her arm around him. "My parents plan on saving us some for our one-year anniversary. I guess that ensures we'll visit them in Beaumont a year from now."

He kissed her forehead. "We can come back whenever you'd like." He leaned forward for another kiss, but she tugged his arm. Hand-in-hand, he walked with his bride to the parking lot. A 'Just Married' sign hung from the back of his van. Painted cans and pink and purple streamers framed the sign.

He opened the passenger side door for Beth. "After you, Mrs. Graham." He leaned in, kissed her, and got into the vehicle.

Beth fastened her seat belt and looked up at him. "Can we make one more stop before we leave town?"

He caressed the side of her face. "We can do anything you want."

"I'd like to stop by the cemetery. To see Chris."

He nodded in understanding and drove his bride to the other side of town.

From the parking lot, they walked a quarter mile to the cemetery. Beth stopped him as they neared the grave. "I want to say good-bye to him, but if it's too hard for you to do this, I understand."

"No, I want to do this." At least this time when Beth would visit the grave, he'd stand beside her instead of cowering from a distance.

He held his wife as they stood in front of Chris's grave, and an overwhelming sense of peace overtook Mark. The guilt of the past was gone.

Beth released his hold and removed a piece of

jewelry from her pocket.

Mark arched his eyebrows. "Are those what I think they are?"

"I don't need to hold onto them anymore. I can let go." She placed Chris's dog tags on his headstone and released a sigh.

Mark swiped the dog tags. "You can't leave these here. Chris would have wanted you to keep them."

"Are you sure?"

"You should keep them." He put his arm around her and gave her a squeeze. "You can give them to our kids."

Beth blushed.

"I'm serious." Mark pressed the dog tags into her palm. "You can tell our children about their uncle and how he fought bravely."

Beth leaned into his shoulder as they walked back to the car.

Once inside the vehicle, she turned toward him. "Are you about ready to start that fun summer you promised?" Beth winked.

He revved the van's engine. "Yes, ma'am, I am."

Thank you for purchasing this Harbourlight title. For other inspirational stories, please visit our on-line bookstore at www.pelicanbookgroup.com.

For questions or more information, contact us at customer@pelicanbookgroup.com.

Harbourlight Books
The Beacon in Christian Fiction™
an imprint of Pelican Ventures Book Group
www.pelicanbookgroup.com

May God's glory shine through
this inspirational work of fiction.

AMDG